ALIETTE DE BODARD

IN THE
VANISHERS' PALACE

ALSO BY ALIETTE DE BODARD

OBSIDIAN AND BLOOD
*Servant of the Underworld**
*Harbinger of the Storm**
*Master of the House of Darts**

DOMINION OF THE FALLEN
The House of Shattered Wings
The House of Binding Thorns

XUYA UNIVERSE
On a Red Station, Drifting
*The Citadel of Weeping Pearls**
*The Tea Master and the Detective^*

SHORT FICTION
Of Books, and Earth, and Courtship

* available as a JABberwocky ebook worldwide
^ available as a JABberwocky ebook outside of North
America

ALIETTE DE BODARD

IN THE
VANISHERS' PALACE

Published by JABberwocky Literary Agency, Inc.

IN THE VANISHERS' PALACE
by Aliette de Bodard

Cover art © 2018 by Kelsey Liggett
Cover layout by Melanie Ujimori and
Rhiannon Rasmussen-Silverstein

Copyright © 2018 by Aliette de Bodard
Published in 2018 by JABberwocky Literary Agency, Inc., in association
with the Zeno Agency LTD.

www.awfulagent.com/ebooks

ISBN 978-1-625673-98-5

ONE

Fish, Gate, River, Storm

The first inkling that things were going wrong was when the voices in Oanh's room fell silent.

To Yên and Mother, Oanh should have been one patient out of many, another risk of infection and loss. And Heaven knew they lost so many of the sick, in the days after the breaking of the world, when medicine was a slow, laborious thing, and the few words of power the Broken-World Teacher had rediscovered didn't make for more than painstaking stopgaps. But Oanh was Yên's friend. The sight of her, shivering and pale in a bed so large and soft it seemed to be crushing her into insignificance, had tightened a fist around Yên's innards until Mother—with one look at Yên's still figure—imperiously sent her out of the room.

"You'll call—" Yên had said.

"If I need you. Yes." Mother leant on her cane with a snort. "Now go."

Yên went outside without demurring, and listened to low voices from inside the room—questions asked, pulses taken, khi-elements around and inside the body numbered and weighed. The wooden floors were rough under the thin, frayed silk of her robes, and a faint smell of jasmine mingled with rot filled the dark space under the rafters. The few lanterns on the wall and on the low lacquered tables were not sufficient to keep the shadows away.

Then silence. Not an abrupt thing, but a slow fading of noise. A question asked. A hesitant answer, and nothing more. Had Mother decided to cast a spell? Surely there was something she could do, to cast out the virus?

Voices outside, familiar ones. And a different kind of silence: that of deference and fear. "I hope we're not too late."

"Don't be a fool. We came as soon as we knew."

The village elders. Yên rose, hastily rearranging her rumpled, stained dress. Not that she could do much about the reek of camphor and menthol ointment, or the red and black ink staining the faded embroidery.

They filed into the room, one by one: their clothes rich and colorful, their wrinkled faces in shadow, magnified and stretched until they hardly seemed human anymore. No, they were human. The worst of what it meant to be human, self-serving and greedy, expecting thoughtless, craven respect. A faint smell of sandalwood wafted to Yên's nostrils, with a sour, unpleasant aftertaste.

"Child," Elder Minh Tho said. She was the eldest of them, and the one who spoke for them all. Her voice was calm and measured, as it always was, even when sentencing someone to exile or death. "I see you're still helping your mother."

"Helping the village," Yên said. She kept her voice slow, as measured as Elder Tho's. Elder Tho ranked everything in terms of use, and Yên was the epitome of useless in her world: a failed scholar, teaching the children reading skills not indispensable to the village's survival; an indifferent healer's assistant, nothing more than a set of hands to prepare bandages or mix ointments.

"A much-appreciated skill," Elder Tho said. Her smile revealed sharp, pointed teeth, like a predator's.

She was here because of Oanh. They all were. Of course they'd never come all this way in the dead of the night for an ordinary person, for Yên or Mother or any of the children Yên taught. But Oanh's mother, Phuoc, was head of the village. Phuoc and Oanh, unlike Mother and Yên, were valuable. Valued and not forced to eke out a living with the constant fear they'd no longer be found useful, that they'd be cast into the wilderness to be taken apart by the Vanishers' constructs, or infected by their plagues. Or worse, labelled as troublemakers and purified in the Plague Grove: slowly taken apart by the Vanisher artefact there under the eyes of the entire village.

Yên forced herself not to move, to remain bowing and submissive. "She's inside."

From the bedroom, a tinkle of beads as Oanh's mother drew the curtain. Her face was pale, and the makeup didn't quite hide the grey circles under her eyes. She gestured the elders in, in odd, dreadful silence. None of the elders spoke as they walked into Oanh's room.

Other whispers. Yên couldn't help it. She had to know what was happening. The elders and Head Phuoc in the same room with Mother meant nothing good for Mother. Mother, of course, would never see it that way: she'd long accepted that one day her luck would run out and she'd be exiled to die. She'd tried to teach Yên about respect and graceful acceptance of one's fate. Yên, though, knew it wasn't luck but the elders' amused forbearance. And no one should ever have to depend on that to live. She crept closer to the door.

"You're proposing to call myths to life." Elder Tho said. "We all know what the cost of that is."

"It's for Oanh." Head Phuoc's voice was low and intense. "For my child."

Mother's voice, not loud, but slow and ponderous, the way she was when making a decision. "It's the only way."

Silence. Then someone moved closer to the curtain. Too close. Yên withdrew, far enough that she'd look to be plausibly fiddling with the mortar and pestle if anyone came in.

Myths. Legends. Before the world broke, they might have been comforts; but now everything was twisted and distorted, and spirits killed without so much as a warning. Mother couldn't—

Before she could think, she was up and at the curtain again, and ran straight into someone.

Elder Giang.

They wore brocade with dragons and ky lân flowing across the large sleeves, an intricate piece passed down in the family, generation after generation, from the single ancestor who had been a scholar-magician. They held Yên effortlessly, pushing her back into the room, step by step. Not that they needed to, for they could simply have summoned guards to take her away. "Child."

Yên caught her breath. She looked down, to not be accused of disrespect, though Giang had always been kinder to her than most elders. "I heard—"

Giang's angular face was very still. They were the youngest of the elders, ascended to the council because their family still had the wealth of their scholar-magician ancestors, and their wife's relatives held most of the land around the river. "Then you'll know to stay out of the way."

"I can't—"

From beyond the curtain came a low humming. Mother's voice, in what seemed to be a prayer but became the familiar accents of a litany, words of power strung together with the same care as beads on a necklace.

Fish. Gate. River. Storm. Come. Fish, gate, river . . .

The curtain shifted colors. It was slow and subtle, but the rising feeling in Yên's chest wasn't. It was that familiar tightness, the sense that something within her was trying to work its way loose and cared little whether it tore her lungs out in the process. Magic. The Broken-World Teacher's words: she could see them, syllables glowing with the iridescence of the diseased river, bright colors dotted with faded blue streaks like rot. *Fish. Gate. River. Storm.* Her own aptitude for magic was nonexistent, but she was a scholar, and she could still read them. She could feel them in the air, in the tiles beneath her, a low thrumming that spread from the room into Yên and Elder Giang—and then beyond, toward the village's scattered houses, the river and the darker shape of the Plague Grove.

Fish, gate, river, storm.

The thrumming grew and then sharpened, as if a line, thrown taut, had suddenly caught. A shiver traveled up Yên's spine. At the doors, the words flared: not going lighter or brighter, but, for a moment only, stretching to another shape, making the Broken-World Teacher's words alien and incomprehensible.

And then it was all gone, but the feeling of tautness remained, as though they were on the edge of a storm. Elder Giang released Yên: their face was flushed, and their expression . . .

Yên wasn't used to seeing it on the elders' faces, but she knew it because it was her own. It was fear, and not just any fear: the fear of losing what you held dear, the idea that everything—your life, your dear ones—could be so much dust on nothing more than another's whim.

Spirits killed.

Something . . . something was wrong. It took her a moment to realize that it was the floor under her, that it was vibrating, not strongly, not shaking, but merely giving them a distant echo of someone coming closer.

"Elder—"

Giang shook their head. The beaded curtain had been pulled back, and Elder Tho was waiting, her wrinkled face unreadable. She didn't even seem to see Yên. For once, she had no contempt, and no subtle or unsubtle reminder of how Yên was a burden on the village. Her entire attention was focused on what was coming. The floorboards under Yên were vibrating again, a low-key buzzing that would start and stop every few minutes. Footsteps.

Unlike Yên's house, Head Phuoc's had an outside door: the walls of a compound around it, and lacquered gates with peeling outer layers, all guarded. No matter how large the spirit was, they should have been stopped, or the guards should have been talking, or taking up escort.

Instead, the door opened.

"I am here," a voice like the thunder of the sea said.

In its wake, nothing but a rippling, stifling silence. Yên had expected something large and monstrous, but it was merely a person standing on the threshold, bathed in the radiance of the diseased moon in the ragged skies. A woman: she'd used the feminine to refer to herself.

She was small and slight. Yên, malnourished as a child, had always been smaller than her comrades, and the woman was only slightly taller than her. But she held herself effortlessly with the decisiveness of authority and power. Scales mottled her skin and hands, and her fingers were curved and sharp, slightly too splayed out. Her hair was tied in a scholar's topknot, the hairsticks holding it in place bare lengths of unadorned wood. Her clothes were dark, utilitarian silk: the dye that of the wealthy, uniform with no bleeding.

Her gaze swept the room, stopping for a bare moment not on Elder Giang but on Yên, and in her eyes, Yên saw the contained fury of the river's storms, the floods that killed, the cold that froze bones until they shattered.

Fish, river, gate, storm.

Dragon.

Yên's words seemed to have deserted her. She pointed, wordlessly, to the room where Oanh lay, where Mother and the elders waited. *Ancestors, keep them safe. Please. Please.*

The woman nodded, and walked away without a word. Her robes—the cloth was ordinary, but they trailed as she moved, halfway between a tail and a spread of cloth—and in the vast blackness that followed her, Yên saw the sweep of words. Not the Broken-World Teacher's script, but something that could have been its ancestor, as Classical had been to Viêt before both languages diverged. Magic. The letters shifted and changed, the alphabet almost but not quite familiar, tantalizingly close to words Yên could make out.

Elder Giang breathed out. The sound broke the silence, but not the tension in the room.

Once, dragons had watched over rivers and rain, dispensed floods, protected villages—drowned, sometimes, but only when Heaven willed it. Once, they had been fair and just. But the Vanishers had poisoned the world and left, and everything had twisted and died in their wake, spirits included.

"She'll be fine. Your mother—"

"You can't know that," Yên said.

Behind the closed door came voices she couldn't hear. She was desperate to move close once again, to know what was going on. A price to pay, the elders had said. She'd heard the stories from other villages. It'd be the summoner or the sick person or both, depending on the dragon's whim. Mother or Oanh. Too much to hope it would be the elders, but of course they would sacrifice anyone else if it allowed them to wriggle out. Elder Giang, perhaps not, but Elder Giang was too young to have much influence yet.

"She's been a healer for decades, hasn't she?"

Yên shook her head. Mother used magic but didn't summon spirits. Too dangerous. But, when the life of the head's child was at stake . . . For the first time, it occurred to her that this mightn't be about her friend, but about the consequences of letting the daughter of a powerful woman die. "It's unfair," she said, before her brain could stop her mouth.

Elder Giang chose not to notice. "Trust your mother, child."

Trust wasn't the issue. Yên did trust Mother. Oanh too, though Oanh was too sick to matter much; she'd always stood up for Yên with the village's other children. And that was all the people Yên trusted. Most of all, the woman—the dragon—Yên trusted only to follow her nature.

Light flared in the slit between the threshold and the door: a soft slow radiance like an underwater sun. In its wake, shadows spread, the same blackness that had followed the woman, gently filling the available space. No. Yên turned toward the open door of the house and saw that the blackness didn't stop. It went on, growing fainter and fainter, toward the gates of the compound, towards the river. It wasn't new. It had been there since the woman had come, but now it was dark enough to be visible. In its depths glimmered the words that Yên had already seen, the ones she could almost read. That one looked like a more complex version of "duty", this other one like a stylized version of "growth", this one like "dreams" or "thoughts" . . . .

She shook her head. What was she thinking? The words were hypnotic, but they weren't the focus. She should be thinking of Mother, of what could be happening in that room. "Please," she said to Elder Giang. "If I could come in . . ."

Elder Giang shook their head. "Do you want to disturb *her*?" It was clear who they meant.

If it meant saving Mother's life . . . Yên bit her tongue to prevent the disrespectful words from escaping her. If nothing else, Mother would remind her to respect older people, but none of this applied to those who made both of them live in fear for personal gain.

The light died. For a moment, a single agonized, suspended moment, no noise came out, but surely they would have screamed if any of them had been harmed? Yên pushed at Elder Giang again, but Giang wouldn't budge.

The door opened. The dragon walked out, but not alone. She was holding Mother's limp shape in her arms. The words Yên had seen in her wake had now climbed up her arms, and the same light, too, danced on Mother's own arms and hands, luminous text swimming like shoals of fish beneath her skin. *No*—Yên's heart was in her throat—something gave in her, and with a strength she didn't know she had, she pushed Elder Giang aside, to stand in the dragon's path. Beneath her, the darkness had faded, but the words were still there, gently drifting in and out of shape as the dragon walked toward Yên.

For a while they faced each other in silence. *Let her go, please. She's all I have,* Yên wanted to say, but the words were too trite, or too biting, or both. The dragon's gaze was unreadable. The storm swirled in her pupils, pulling at something in Yên's chest.

"Here," the dragon said. She held out Mother to Yên. Yên took her, arms bowing under the weight. Mother was old and frail, but to carry her as effortlessly as the dragon had . . . "She's exhausted herself summoning me," the dragon went on. There was no emotion in her voice.

Yên opened her mouth and tried to speak, but found no words in the scorched desert of her heart.

"Take care of her," the dragon said. "I'll be back."

And, without a further word, or even a further glance, she walked out of the house. Oily, glimmering darkness followed in her wake, a mirror of the diseased skies above.

* * *

Elder Giang helped Yên bring Mother home. She got the sense that it was as much to help her as because they didn't want to face what had happened in the room. They'd both seen Oanh, briefly: lying in that too-large bed, her breathing slow and steady, and no longer labored. The spots of color on her cheeks had subsided. She didn't look *healthy*, per se: the luminous words in the dragon's wake still clung to her wrists, a faint imprint like bracelets that looked as though it'd scar. Her skin . . .her skin was almost gone, as if the dragon had flayed her but still left her—barely—breathing. Her eyes were sunken deep into their orbits, her entire being subtly altered, so that everything seemed keener, more clearly defined as if pared away by the edge of a knife, cheekbones prominent, lips thinned, her black hair failing to hide her shoulder blades thrusting upward, through the waste of her skin. Yên had squeezed her hands: the pulse was back and strong, but she'd felt veins and muscles beating and rippling under her fingers.

"She needs to rest," Elder Tho had said, smiling that toothy smile of hers, the one that promised bad things.

"She'll be better soon," Head Minh Phuoc had said, sounding for all the world as though she didn't believe it.

Oanh was alive, and the fever had broken. She was changed, but surely change was such a small price to pay for keeping the demons of death at bay? Had the change been the dragon's price? Surely not. It seemed far too insignificant.

As Yên and Elder Giang laid Mother on her small bed,

she woke up, and looked straight through Yên. The glazed, slightly distant expression scared Yên to death: a hint of wonder and awe, soft feelings that, in the world after the departure of the Vanishers, just got people killed. "Mother—"

"It worked. I saw her."

"I saw her too. Mother, what did she ask for?"

"Child." A soft exhalation that barely warmed up Yên's hand. "She was so beautiful . . ." And then she closed her eyes, and slept again. Her skin was drained and translucent, the wrinkles on her face deep furrows like the ones in the diseased, ravaged earth outside. The ink of the dragon's summoning still stained the skin beneath her fingernails. The words Yên had seen, the words that had still been clinging to Oanh, seemed to be gone. The dragon was right: she needed rest. The thought was a stone in Yên's mind.

The dragon had said she'd come back. What for, and when?

Elder Giang stayed for a while, hovering at the door as though they wanted to tell Yên something but couldn't quite work out what. Their gaze was fearful. Fragile. Unusual for an elder, even more unusual for them. Yên no longer had the energy to dance around village politics, if she'd ever had it. She'd only learned to do it because Mother was so hopelessly uninterested by it. "Do you want tea?" she asked.

She'd expected them to make their excuses and leave, but much to her surprise, they nodded, and helped her draw water from the beaten-down purification unit. They sat cross-legged at the low table, breathing in the grassy, soft smell of the tea, with the kind of easy grace that belonged at court.

The children Yên taught had made an effort to clean up after class, though Vinh, as usual, had left a pile of open books and calligraphy papers dangerously close to the teapot. Yên surreptitiously nudged them out of the way, using the opportunity to flip them over. She wasn't sure if Elder Giang would have approved of Vinh's habit of drawing plants and fish in the margins of her essays—no matter how beautiful they were, the animals effortlessly flowing alongside the calligraphied letters.

"You tried the Metropolitan exam last year," Elder Giang said.

Yên flushed. She hadn't thought she would. "I failed." It would have been her and Mother's way out of the village. To go to the capital under armed escort as a meritorious scholar, to be presented to the Empress and her consort; to be, if not rich, then at least favored. Valued. Not to be thrown away on a whim. They could have slept, knowing that they would never be taken away to the Plague Grove to be slowly taken apart by the purifying artefact. Yên still had nightmares from the last time she'd been forced to attend a purification: old Thanh Hoa, looking across the circle as light fell into shimmering veils around her, locking her into place—her skin lifting itself from glistening muscles, and muscles and veins from bones, and then the bones themselves peeling away, discarded layer after layer, and an endless, impossible scream bursting from lips and vocal cords flayed away into nothingness . . . .

In the capital, Yên and Mother could have slept, knowing that they were safe. Away from Elder Tho and her endless, predatory waiting. "I'll try again," Yên said. "In three years' time."

"It's an admirable attempt," Giang said, at last. There was no irony in their voice. "I tried that, when I was young. Running away from the village as soon as I could."

They had a secure position in the order of things—their family rich and influential, their lands vital to the village's food supply.

They'd never had to worry about survival, or how desirable they were. "Things were different, when you were young," Yên said, cautiously. What was Elder Giang trying to say?

Elder Giang sighed. "The next exam is in three years' time." They sipped their tea, slowly. "Sometimes, the best thing to do isn't waiting."

"I don't understand," Yên said.

"You want me to tell you it will get better," Giang said. "But it will get worse, child. And"—they stared at their cup for a while—"three years is a lifetime."

They were clear. Too clear, to the point of bluntness. "You want us to leave now. Mother healed Oanh—" If that wasn't value to the village, then what was?

Elder Giang drained their cup and rose. "Let me be blunt, then. It's not Mother who needs to leave."

Yên stared at them. She wasn't stupid. "The dragon's price."

"She asked for a life," Elder Giang said. "Oanh's life, but . . ." They let the word hang in the air, its meaning all too clear.

Yên was many things. But even befuddled and struggling to follow a conversation, she wasn't stupid. She was the one in danger. Whatever life the dragon had asked for, in the end, it had fallen on her. Of course. "I can't leave," she said. "Mother."

"I can take care of your mother." Elder Giang gave her that look again: brittle and haunted, as though something fundamental in them had broken in that room. "You need to run."

"Now?"

Elder Giang's face was hard. "I tried, child. I did. But sometimes things are rotted through. Like a cancer."

"I can't run now," Yên said. "Not at night." At night, with the Vanishers' leftover constructs prowling the forests outside the village? She wasn't old or lame like Mother, but she'd still be torn apart anyway. And where would she run to? What other village would take her in, when she had nothing to bring other than vague knowledge of letters and healing?

But it wasn't as if she had a choice. She'd have to grab things before running away, because they would watch the house afterward. She'd need food and drink: tea, rice cakes, some of Mother's unguents for the most urgent of wounds. The thought of leaving without even time to say her goodbyes to Mother, of trying to argue with another set of elders how much she was worth, just made her feel nauseous. "How much time do I have?"

Elder Giang spread their hands. "I don't know," they said.

Yên owned little: thin brushes, brittle paper, diluted ink, and the broken shards of an inkstone, the treasures of a moneyless scholar. A tunic and trousers of rough, threadbare silk, the embroidered peaches mere circles of color on a tree barren of leaves and branches. Not much to pack, but then, she didn't have time for sentimentality. "Let me just—" she started, and then she heard the noise outside the house.

A simple curtain was the only thing that separated their door from the village streets. Other houses had thick metal doors, and identity controls salvaged from Vanisher artefacts, but neither Mother nor Yên could afford such things. They'd always known the truth: anything that made it past the village's armored walls and sentinels would make short work of metal or wood.

Elder Giang's face was tight. "I thought we had more time." They moved to stand in front of Yên as though they could ward off the inevitable, and threw open the curtain. Yên followed them, her heart beating madly in her chest. It didn't feel real. Too sudden and too unexpected. It was happening. As she'd always known it would.

Outside, at the bottom of the steps leading to their house, a circle of village elders, grave and solemn. And Elder Tho, pale-skinned and tall, in the pale light of the pockmarked, diseased moon. "Younger pibling," she said, sharply, to Elder Giang, making an imperious gesture with her hand. Her displeasure was clear in the way she addressed Giang: not to a younger but still-respected sibling, but simply with the neutral term for parent's sibling, the formal one reserved for strangers.

Elder Giang said, softly, slowly, drawing themself up to their full height, "This isn't right."

Elder Tho's face didn't move. "This is how it has always been, younger pibling. The weak die so that we may survive."

"The weak." Elder Giang's face was unreadable. "Do you really think a healer's daughter and apprentice is weak and useless?"

"Enough," Elder Tho said. "I can also have you removed." The way she said it suggested something far more permanent than calling the militia on Elder Giang. And, to Yên: "Don't make this harder than it has to be, child. It could be your mother instead of you."

A memory, unbidden: Mother, hanging pale and limp in the dragon's hands, the words of light lazily whirling beneath her skin, going fainter every time they crossed under the bones. Mother, going away with the darkness forever. No. "The village needs a healer," Yên said, all thoughts of respect and decorum fleeing her.

"Are you questioning our decisions?"

"The First Teacher said one should never be afraid to correct one's mistakes," Yên said. She had Elder Giang in front of her on the steps, and saw them flinch at the bluntness and disrespect of this. But really, didn't they know where it was going? Just as Elder Tho could remove Giang, she could as easily remove Yên.

"Don't make a fuss, child. That is unbecoming of you."

Mother. Elder Tho had never liked her or Mother, and no matter how self-destructive it might be for the village. She'd smile and say that diseases killed anyway, that there were other scholars who knew the words of the Broken-World Teacher, never mind that none of them knew how to apply them to healing.

Being rude would get her nowhere. They'd already decided, but they were reluctant to make a scene unless they absolutely had to. And she could use that to bargain for scraps.

The thought was as bitter as ashes in her mouth.

Yên said, slowly, "Mother is old and wise, and I'm her only support. If I go away, would someone take care of her?"

"I've told you," Elder Giang said. They sounded exhausted. "I'll take care of your mother."

Yên looked, unblinkingly, at Elder Tho. Because she needed to hear Tho say it. Not a promise—she wouldn't be able to trust it—but something from her. Anything.

Scraps. Crumbs.

"It will be arranged," Elder Tho said, smoothly. "We're not suggesting that filial piety be trampled. But the village has incurred a debt, and it has to be paid."

A debt. A life given to the dragon, and everyone knew

what dragons did with the lives of mortals. At best, she'd be dead; at worse, a plaything to be broken.

Yên inclined her head. "May I say goodbye?" she asked.

Elder Tho frowned. "We have no time—" Something in Elder Giang's face must have stopped her, because although Giang didn't say anything, they suddenly seemed to grow taller yet, filled with the wrath of Heaven.

"Filial piety," Elder Giang said, simply. A single word in Viêt.

Elder Tho didn't move, but she relaxed, a fraction. "Not long, then," she said, grudgingly.

2

The Heart of the River

Mother woke up, only for long enough for Yên to kiss her. She sank back immediately into sleep afterward, and Yên wasn't even sure if Mother would remember this upon waking. Yên could only hope, could only pray to dead ancestors for a mercy that had long since departed from the world. Even the Vanishers hadn't known what the word meant. They had been cruel and fey, taking what they pleased to build their artefacts and gates and ships. Mercy was something Yên's ancestors had had to teach themselves, to remember that they were different.

In the end, Yên left a message to Mother in the house: broad strokes hurriedly written on a scrap of paper she wedged under her empty teacup. What could one say to one's own mother? Every word seemed too small, too slight to say what Yên wanted to say: *please live. Please grow older and wiser, and recognized. Please.*

And the words she couldn't put on paper, lying heavy on her heart: *I always thought you would go first. It's unfair, parents shouldn't have to bury their own children. Please forgive me. I was given no choice.*

One small mercy to be thankful for: it was night, and all the children were in bed. They wouldn't have to watch—because of course they'd have had to, just as every purification was a public occurrence. They'd wake up and find Yên gone, and forget her in time. Though she hoped Vinh's parents would remember what she'd said, and encourage Vinh to sit for the examinations: the nine-year-old had true talent, the kind that would blossom into scholarship if properly tended to. A small pinch of regret that she'd never see that, or find out if Khiêm would ever learn to sit still and listen, or if Thiên An would understand she needed to take more risks in her essays and in her life.

They would be fine. They were the village's future, and not even Elder Tho would dare to cut those lives short.

Elder Tho and the others escorted Yên to the edge of the Plague Grove, outside the village's walls. There'd been a debate on whether they should put on isolation skins, but Elder Tho had cut it short: they couldn't offend the dragon by implying she might be contagious. So, the skins remained in the village. Elder Giang looked, for a moment, in danger of being sent back to the village, but Elder Tho grudgingly allowed them to come with Yên. They walked in silence, not saying a word, until they reached the Plague Grove.

It was away from the village: a place for travelers to be quarantined if necessary. The trees were skeletal and thin.

Silver circles of words surrounded them, generations of scholar-magicians inscribing wards of protection for the village's safety in the ground until the paint itself seemed to have become part of the earth. In the center was the purifying artefact, mercifully silent and dark. At least Yên wasn't going there. At least it would be over soon, except that she couldn't even be sure of that.

Yên stood, shivering, in the trees by the river's side. A smell of sheening oil and rot wafted from the polluted water. Light shone beneath the surface, dancing in abstract patterns. The skeletal, hollow moon limned the gnawed, diseased branches in dim grey light. By Yên's side were the village elders, ghostly, almost-featureless figures in the moon's light. Elder Tho held Yên's wrist tight enough to bruise. "She's late," Elder Tho said, sounding annoyed.

Yên wasn't sure if late made a difference—a few more moments of freedom, a few more moments of breathing—because who knew why the dragon had asked for a life?

"Elder sister." Elder Giang's voice was tinny and muffled as they spoke. "Please be quiet. At night—"

Yên could have laughed, if she'd still had laughter in her. Of course, they were outside the village boundaries at night, and Heaven only knew what waited for them under the trees.

"Perhaps we should have taken your mother," Elder Tho said.

Yên forced out words from between frozen lips. "You promised . . ." But what was the value of promises, to women such as her? Elder Tho had always gotten her own

23

way. She had always had the village bend to her will and whims, and an impoverished scholar like Yên weighed so little in her world.

To Yên's surprise, Elder Tho shook her head. "I did." Her voice was low and thoughtful. "We made a bargain, and I'll hold to it. If you do."

"You know I have no choice," Yên said. She bit her lip. Respect, she had to remember respect, but she was tired of bowing to her own death.

Elder Tho's mouth opened—to censure, to order every bone in Yên's body broken—but Elder Giang spoke up first. "Elder sister, the river!"

In the water, the luminous stains had stopped drifting: they swirled around a motionless center, as if someone had planted a brush into the river's bed and turned, again and again, a slowly increasing frenzy of stains and blobs all merging into one another, a congealing mass of light shot through with holes like a lotus root hollowed out of seeds. No, not a mass of light: they were *words*, the same ones that had trailed the dragon as she'd come into the village. *Duty. Dreams. Worship.*

The light dimmed, throwing into sharp relief the boundaries between letters. The words drifted slightly apart as if something, holding its breath and drawing them all in, had suddenly released it.

Something pushed from beneath the water—emerging, lithe and sinuous, a huge, serpentine body, translucent stubs of antlers with the same glow as the moon's—a mane, scattering droplets of river water as the dragon shook herself, her roar the thunder of a storm that stripped leaves and bark from the trees. Teeth—sharp, pointed—gleamed in her mouth, and it took no effort at all to imagine that huge maw snapping over flesh and bone, tearing chunks of meat away from arms and legs, nudging ribs open to gobble up heart and liver and lungs.

Mother had been right: she was beautiful.

Yên should have been on her knees like the elders, face pressed to the ground, hiding from this luminous, terrible creature to whom she now belonged, from her death and all the stretched hours that would come before it. But she couldn't look away.

The dragon stretched, body arching upward, a line of scales pointing straight to the lambent sky; and then bent forward again, head making straight for the shore, gaining speed, as if she meant to scoop Yên up in her jaws. Yên, sluggish and entranced, watched her come: light coalescing on pearlescent scales, droplets of water shaken to the ground like a shower of jade and silver, eyes as large as her hands, the dark pupils like a hole into which she was endlessly falling—

The light shifted, hardened. The dragon shimmered, and shrank. For a bare moment, she was two things in the same place. And then the serpentine body faded, and only the shape of a human remained.

It was the same person Yên had already seen: unchanged, though her face was tight with an expression Yên couldn't name. Eagerness, blood-thirst?

Ancestors . . .

The dragon walked to where Yên was standing, slowly, leisurely. Around Yên, the air tightened, turning cold and wet. Tendrils of mist rose from the ground, smelling musty, clamping themselves around Yên's limbs and face until she could no longer move.

"Well, well," the dragon said. She put a hand under Yên's chin. Her touch was wet and slimy, but the mist tendrils held Yên, as she'd have jerked away. "What do we have here?" The dragon lifted Yên's face, held it for a while. "My payment for a healing?"

Her eyes were the color of a storm, never quite holding a shade or nuance, blue and green and grey in a dizzying dance, and the pupils were the dragon's, dark and bottomless. Even if Yên had been free, even if she could have moved, she'd have remained there, staring into them until she was lost.

"You're not the human I healed," the dragon said. She still held Yên's face, with both hands on either side of her cheeks now, lightly pressing down, as if debating whether to crush it between their palms. "You're the summoner's daughter."

"Honored lady," Elder Tho said. She'd risen from her own bow. She held herself tightly, the shaking of her hands and chest barely noticeable, though the dragon knew. Had to know. "She offered herself to replace Oanh, the child you healed."

The dragon let go of Yên but didn't stop looking at her. Weighing her. Wondering what she was worth, what her life or death would be worth? "She offered herself.

Did she, now." She nodded toward Yên, and the tendrils around Yên snapped out of existence. "Well?"

Yên swallowed, her breath burning in her throat, and saw Elder Tho's steely gaze. A bargain, to keep Mother safe. She had to. "Oanh is a friend," she said. A friend who slept, exhausted and changed, and would never notice Yên was gone until it was too late. Every word felt like a red-hot pebble in Yên's throat. Mother. She had to think of Mother. Better her life than Mother's. "She's got a bright future ahead of her, and I"—she breathed in, slowly, carefully—"I don't."

"Indeed not." The dragon seemed amused: a thin parting of the lips to reveal teeth too sharp to be human, a smile that went nowhere near her eyes. She turned to Elder Tho. "You offer her to me as a replacement for Oanh? Did you not think of getting the summoner here?"

"I—I don't—" Elder Tho started, flustered.

"Don't take me for a fool." The dragon's voice was low, pleasant. "I can feel this one's heartbeat in my hands. She's not the one who chose to come here."

Elder Giang spoke up. "Yên's mother is old and infirm. Surely, her life is of no value—"

"You offer me youth and beauty instead of knowledge?" The dragon laughed, a thunderous sound that turned Yên's legs to jelly. She fought not to fall to her knees. "Do you think I need a child"—she spat out the word—"to warm my bed?"

Yên heard the words from far away; she felt the blood leave her face, leaving her shaking and weak. She hadn't thought—she'd thought she might suffer and die, but not that. Never that.

The dragon moved away from her, toward the elders and Elder Tho, who now stood rooted to the ground, held by the same threads of mist that had held Yên. She paused, the folds of her silk tunic billowing in a rising wind. In the distance, a construct howled. "You aren't worthy of this village," she said, in that same pleasant tone, which suggested she'd be equally happy slaughtering them where they stood. "You"—she laid a hand against Elder Tho's chest, pushed until Elder Tho turned as pale as rice paper, the shaking of her hands visible, her knees sinking from under her—"pleading and promising and threatening, to save your own above all others. "And you"—to the other elders, as she passed them one by one, laying one hand on each of their foreheads in turn, where a word glimmered the color of the river, shimmering with the reflections of spilled oil—"cowards letting this happen rather than holding her in check."

She walked back to Yên calmly, while behind her the elders sank to their knees, as if they'd cut the strings holding them. Elder Tho remained standing, but growing paler and paler, her eyes the only things alive in the whole of her face. Elder Giang was struggling to pull themself to their knees, though in their eyes Yên saw nothing of fear or pleading, but merely acceptance of something they'd known was coming.

"Please," Yên said. She could have asked for Giang's life, but what would that make of her, if she played the same game of favorites as Elder Tho?

The dragon watched her, for a while, eyes like holes in the oval of her face. "What's your name?"

"Yên. Hai Yên."

"Sea swallow." The dragon sounded amused. "I won't kill them," she said, mildly. "Come."

"Where?"

The dragon raised a thin, dark eyebrow. Dull scales moved across her left cheek, slowly spreading to armor her neck. Yên fought an impulsive, foolish urge to touch them. "I claimed your life. And, in any case, would you stay in your village, after what's happened here? There would be . . . repercussions. Unpleasant ones."

Yên forced herself to move. Her legs wouldn't obey her. After what felt like an eternity, she finally managed to unglue one foot from the muddy earth, under the dragon's visibly growing impatience. "I have family . . ." She'd have said *friends*, but the only name that came to her mouth was Oanh's.

"Yes," the dragon said. "In a foreign, faraway land you can't come back to." She walked toward the river, growing as she did so, lengthening until she was once more the serpentine, elegant shape that had burst out of the water. Her tail wrapped around Yên's waist, loosely— that same wet and slimy feeling, except this time Yên managed to hold herself still as it seeped through her clothes.

In the river, the words appeared again, danced and coalesced until everything seemed awash with a radiance stronger than the moon's.

The dragon dived into the center of the river, taking Yên with her.

* * *

Yên woke up with a headache. She sat up slowly, and realized something was wrong. She should have seen the ceiling of the sleeping alcove: instead, there was a wall, somewhere farther in the distance. That wasn't an exaggeration, because the room she was in was huge. The same kind of odd letters she'd seen glowing in the water ran down the side of the bed she was lying in. As they went farther, they altered and shifted orientation, and the walls of the room turned with them and expanded, the unknown words multiplying, turning and growing until they blurred somewhere in an infinite distance, a vertiginous effect that made Yên clutch the sides of the bed for reassurance—look away, she had to look away lest she be drawn into a chasm that had no end.

"Hey, she's awake!"

"Will you look at that!"

A patter of feet on tiles, and then someone jumped at Yên. The bed bounced and creaked under their weight, and before she could even so much as react, she went down in a flurry of limbs and clothes, flailing to recover her balance.

"So much fun!"

Two voices, both too young and lacking the poise of the dragon's. Yên grabbed one arm at random, feeling scales shift under her fingers, and pushed. "Will you let me breathe." She used her teacher's voice, the one for unruly children who refused to learn their alphabet. "Now."

A snort and a grunt. Her assailants quieted down and moved away, and Yên sat up again—*do not look at the walls do not look at the walls.*

There were two of them, sitting on the edge of her bed, lazily dangling legs over the smooth sheets, dressed in flamboyant embroidered silk that shimmered with the light from the room. They looked identical. No, they weren't. Subtle shifts of face and hands—harder to work out, because when they both moved, their faces changed by fragments—revealing antlers in their hair, thin and curled moustaches, a lion's snout instead of a nose. Changing shapes between human and spirit in the blink of an eye. "You're dragons," Yên said, flatly.

Their smiles were dazzling and innocent. "I'm Dan Thông," the one on the left said.

"And I'm Dan Liên," her sibling said. "I'm the younger one." And, in the face of Yên's obvious confusion: "We're your new students!"

The dragon. Yên struggled to remember what had happened after the river. Her mind threw up nothing except darkness, gradually closing in. "I'm going to need some time—"

A door opened. Yên made the mistake of looking up, and saw it lying at a right angle from her current position; and, through the doorframe, a corridor where every wall had windows opening on the vastness of stars. Oh, ancestors, she was going to be sick . . . .

Aliette de Bodard

"Are you all right? Hey, big sib, did they eat anything today?" Liên asked.

"She," Thông said, sternly. "Remember? Mother told us so. And you're not leaving her space to breathe." Thông used gender-neutral pronouns. Liên had an ambiguous appearance and used female ones.

"Children." That was the dragon's voice, sharp and pointed. "Behave. Respect is due to teachers, no matter how mortal they might be." A pause, as her footsteps grew closer, and then, "Especially if they're mortal. They're more easily harmed."

Yên's stomach churned. She gave up on dignity and decorum, and bent over the edge of the bed, throwing up the meager contents of her stomach. The dragon. Ancestors, the dragon was going to kill her—

But she hadn't, had she. What was she waiting for?

When she looked up, the dragon was leaning against one of the bedposts, with that same distant amusement she'd had in the Plague Grove. She wore flowing silk: a stark, black cloth of a shade that Yên had only seen in Vanishers' cloth, with not one clearer patch to mar the deep color. When she moved, it was as if the night sky shifted and spread around her. What would it be like, to have those sleeves enfold Yên—those long, thin fingers wrapped around Yên's shoulders? Yên found her breath catching in her throat again.

Beautiful. No. No. She couldn't afford to think of the dragon that way. She was Yên's master, Yên's executioner. There was no future in desire or love. "You—" Yên swallowed, pulling herself upward, turning away from the vomit on the floor lest she be sick again. "You claimed my life."

The dragon raised an eyebrow.

Yên forced herself to say the words, because she might as well burst the abscess. "Everyone knows dragons kill."

Something passed across the dragon's face, too fast for Yên to see. Pride, anger? "Do they. I'd hate to disappoint them." She raised Yên's face to hers again. Her thin, pointed fingers were claws, though they only lightly rested on Yên's skin, a clammy coldness that should have been trembling on the edge of uncomfortable, spreading to Yên's cheeks and fingers until Yên wasn't sure anymore if it was pain she was shivering with. "You're smart and handsome, and I hate waste," the dragon said, mildly. Yên tried to look away from her eyes, and couldn't. Vertiginous darkness: a hole that swept her away, trembling and struggling to hold herself still and silent, for fear she'd reach out and lose herself in the dragon's gaze.

"Mother," Thông said, their voice tinny, as from a great distance.

The dragon released Yên. "You're a scholar." She turned away, slightly. Yên breathed out—in relief, in disappointment?

"An indifferent one," Yên said. She couldn't help herself. She'd walk to her own death before she'd lie about her own literary achievements, apparently.

The dragon snorted. Oily water hung in the air for a brief moment, sheening with the dimmed colors of diseased rainbows. "Wasted in a small village where literature isn't valued? There's no shame in that." She shook her head. "The twins badly need an education, and you'll provide it to them. I take it they've already introduced themselves to you."

"We can do that again," Liên said, her face shaped in an almost comical frown. Her shape seemed to have stabilized, with only a hint of the dragon when she pulled herself up from the bed. Yên forced herself to stare at the floor rather than at Liên: it made her seem submissive and very un-teacher-like, but if she had to look at the walls, she was going to vomit again.

"Behave," Thông said, sharply.

"Walk with me," the dragon said to Yên, a polite request that was a command. They headed toward that impossible door, the one Yên tried, stubbornly, to look away from. Behind them came noises. It sounded as though Liên and Thông were bundling up Yên's vomit, making quips at each other as they did so. "They're children," the dragon said. "They mean well, but they regularly try to commit suicide. Not a difficult thing to do, in this palace."

"I don't understand," Yên said.

The dragon's voice was mild again. "I didn't build this place. The Vanishers did."

Yên had heard of ships, of gates, and of artefacts, but never of an entire building. "Why?"

"Who knows why the Vanishers did what they did." The dragon snorted again. "It's far too big and far too drafty, but it serves."

If one didn't mind nausea-inducing doors or rooms with improbable geometry. Yên looked up, cautiously. They were at the door, though they couldn't have walked nearly far enough. It was open, the corridor twisting away from them. More letters, this time in shades of metallic red and brown, and open windows on every wall, opening out on a courtyard with caged birds in a small pavilion, against the background of stars. Except that every wall had the pavilion in a different orientation, upward or downward or tilted to the side, as if such things as mundane rules didn't apply.

Ancestors, she was going to be sick again. "You get used to it," the dragon said. "Obviously, their idea of geometry wasn't quite ours."

"You didn't know the Vanishers."

"I'm older than you think," the dragon said. Her voice was still mild, but it had edges now. "We served them, until we no longer had any use."

Yên's face burnt. "I'm sorry. I should have thought—"

"They used everyone." Her body under the dress was growing longer and more serpentine, though her face didn't shift. "As I said, it's an odd thing, to be inhabiting their houses." A revenge, her tone clearly said, if not her words.

Yên said, slowly, carefully, "You could have built another home."

"Yes. It would have been inadequate. I do have responsibilities," the dragon said, and didn't venture anything more. Clearly, she didn't want Yên to ask, and

Yên wasn't brave enough to throw herself at a closed door. "There are places here where your presence isn't appropriate," the dragon went on, in a more relaxed tone.

Yên wasn't surprised. "And forbidden rooms?"

The dragon snorted. "I know mortals. If I forbid you a place, you'll just tear open the doors in your haste to find it. Anyway, you'll find out soon enough, if a place isn't for your use."

She wasn't going to kill Yên. She wanted to use Yên as a teacher; and how hard was it, really, to teach two children? "Because I'll be dead."

"Yes," the dragon said.

"Am I a prisoner, then?" Yên asked. Mother. The village. Giang. Oanh. Mother.

"I did claim your life," the dragon said. "And be fair. Your village elders would have sold you again to the highest bidder. Quite fast, possibly, to remove the memory of their shame from the village."

"They meant well—"

"You know they didn't. Your friend—"

"Elder Giang? They're not my friend," Yên said, more forcefully than she'd meant. Would Elder Giang keep their promise to take care of Mother? Or was it so much empty air?

The dragon shrugged. "All the same to me."

"You were the one who offered the elders the bargain."

"Because no one gets something for nothing," the dragon said. "It sets a bad precedent." She raised an eyebrow. "And, in the end, if you fall to temptation? You only have yourself to blame." Her voice was harsh.

"It's my home!" A small, cramped room, a bed on the floor, the smell of rice over her sleeping mat—the sound of Mother's loud snoring—what she wouldn't have given for this, for any of this, now.

"I told you. It was. In a distant, faraway country. Once touched by the spirits . . ." The dragon exhaled. Then, in a gentler, kinder tone: "You'll get used to it."

"You don't know that I will!"

Again, that distant amusement. "Perhaps I do." And, in a different tone: "Harm a hair on either of the twins, and I'll tear you apart."

They were children. "I wouldn't," Yên said.

"Wouldn't you?" The dragon cocked her head, watching Yên. "Who knows what we'll do, when faced with threats and death?" She sounded amused, ironic again. Her hand was far too close to Yên's, her whole presence an almost-physical weight in the air. Yên braced herself, half-welcoming the touch of that tail again, wrapped around her legs and dragging her on. "Be careful," the dragon said. "In the palace. Or you'll die."

It made little sense to Yên. She latched on to the part that she had understood. "You don't have to care about my well-being."

A pause, and a glance that went on for far too long, devouring her with eyes. "As I said: I hate waste. That doesn't mean you're safe." The dragon gestured to the two small shapes clustered by Yên's bed. "All yours now."

"And if I fail?"

The dragon snorted. "You'll be dead. But most probably because the palace will have killed you, long before I
get around to it."

"Are there—" Yên hesitated, then plunged on, because
she might as well commit herself. "Are there other people
in the palace?"

"Other servants?" The dragon cocked her head.

That wasn't what Yên had wanted to know. Were there
other dragons? One or several spouses? "Other masters,"
she said.

"The Vanishers are gone," the dragon said, sharply,
with a hint of anger.

"I didn't mean to—" But she had, hadn't she? She was
such a fool.

"No." A deep breath, which was the roar of the storm.
"They took much with them," the dragon said, finally.
Her voice was toneless. "But they left all their toys and
pet projects behind. All their diseases, rewriting bodies
and souls as they pleased. You're lucky, out there in the
world. You only see a fraction of them. Here . . . I'm not
warning you about the palace as some empty threat. Spirits can't fight diseases or gene-viruses. There were more of
us, once. Wives. Parents." The words echoed in the silence
of the room, cheap and inadequate to cover what must
have been an ocean of grief.

"I'm sorry."

"Don't be," the dragon said. "What is past is past." But
she sounded as though she would gladly have bitten Yên's

head off, or that of any Vanishers fool enough to venture back into their deserted palace. "Now we look towards the future." She gestured toward the bed, where Thông and Liên were busy arguing with each other, long sleeves streaming in an invisible wind. "Teach them, Yên. Teach them how to survive."

Yên's face burnt. "I will."

"Good." A silence. Then, as Yên turned, to walk back to her new charges: "Yên?"

She turned, found the dragon staring at her in the doorframe of a corridor framed by stars. "There's no point in empty formalities. Let's address each other less ceremoniously, shall we?" She'd shifted pronouns, to something that was just—barely—suitable for master and servant. "My name is Vu Côn."

"Mistress," Yên started, and an invisible wind brushed her lips, silencing her and sending a shiver up her spine.

"Vu Côn," the dragon said. "Remember."

As if she would ever forget.

3

The Dragon's Children

Vu Côn drew the scraping coin along the kidney meridian, all the way from the nape of Diêm Châu's neck to the arch of her foot. It left a reddened trail on the oiled skin: blood, stimulated to flow on the line she'd drawn.

"There," she said. "You can sit up." She dropped the coin in the foundry bowl, where it was taken apart for components. "Let me have a look at your healing spells."

Diêm Châu, wordlessly, held out her arms. The words Vu Côn had written along the biceps' outer edge had faded. She traced them again, carefully. *Flow. Breath. The Sea King's Gift.* They glowed silver for the briefest of moments, before fading to a more tanned color on Diêm Châu's skin.

Diêm Châu said nothing. She was a quiet child: ten years old but behaving herself with the preternatural poise of someone much, much older. Her father had brought her to the palace a moon earlier, but the sickness they'd both contracted had progressed much faster in him, and

Vu Côn had had to put him into permanent sleep, desperately hoping she'd be able to find a spell to cure him. Yên, no doubt, would have expected Vu Côn to kill him, but contrary to legend, she killed the infected only in the outside world—because she had to, because otherwise the world would be overrun by Vanishers' viruses. Diêm Châu, either younger or with a slightly different mutation of the virus, had reacted much better to treatment.

"I'll take you back to your berth," Vu Côn said.

They walked in the corridor, back to the sleepers' room, in silence. "Grandmother . . ." Diêm Châu said, finally, as they reached the door.

"Yes?" Vu Côn said.

"Do you think I'll ever be ready?"

Vu Côn's heart contracted in her chest. She knelt, her face level with Diêm Châu's own, antlers rubbing against Diêm Châu's forehead. For a moment, words failed her. Then she said, "I can't take the sickness out of you right now. But you're getting better. Soon, child. Very soon."

"How soon?"

Vu Côn hated making promises she couldn't keep. But Diêm Châu's face was drawn and tight, and she looked so heartbroken; and who wouldn't, when all her life was stretched, endless time? "One or two sessions."

"Really? And then I'll be healed?"

"Of course," Vu Côn said.

The virus Diêm Châu and her father had contracted was one Vu Côn had seldom seen. She didn't know what its original purpose had been, but it was catalogued as the

41

Occlusion of the Entryways: something that disturbed the skin's balance and threw up rashes faster than she could heal them. Diêm Châu was always flushed, always burning to the touch, and without Vu Côn's regular infusion of healing spells, she'd slip into unconsciousness. Everyone was a balance of âm—the moon part, the quiet, waiting self in the darkness—and duong—the sun part, the forceful light. Diêm Châu's duong was so strong, her âm was barely visible. Vu Côn was trying to rebalance both before she could intervene more durably. Her few patients who'd had it had made a full recovery, but only if she'd properly rebalanced their âm and duong before intervening.

Diêm Châu was silent for a while. "I hate the sleep," she said.

"I know. But without it, you'll die, sweetheart."

Diêm Châu made a face. "Next time. I'll be ready."

"Of course." Vu Côn forced herself to smile at her. "Come on, sweetheart. Time to sleep, now."

After Diêm Châu was back in her stasis berth, among the other sleepers—held in suspended animation so that her symptoms only marginally progressed—Vu Côn walked to her room.

It had been a long, exhausting day. Alone in front of her mirror, Vu Côn undressed, slowly. She was winding down, no longer bothering to maintain one shape. Her hands shifted to claws and back again, half-tearing clothes that the palace would repair in the night, and her skin was becoming dotted, here and there, with iridescent scales. She stared, for a while, at the shadow of antlers at her temples. Hoang would have hated it. He'd always been so prim and proper, as if rules and etiquette, enclosing all they could and could not do, could keep them forever safe.

Of course they couldn't. The Vanishers had made their own rules, and even after they were gone, their palace hadn't meekly bent down to their will—as Hoang had found out, all too late—that even being careful and respectful was no shield against disaster.

A knock at the door tore her from her gloomy thoughts. Thông. They were the only one who knocked that way and waited: Liên just knocked and came in as if expecting everything to be ready for her. "Come in," Vu Côn said.

Thông was worried. It was hard to tell, but Vu Côn had had years to watch them grow up, from a child whose wishes were transparent on their face to this composed young person on the edge of adulthood.

"Liên is in bed," Thông said. "Reading those books again."

Liên had found a treasure trove of mystery books in the library, about a magistrate investigating increasingly bizarre crimes in the provinces of a fictional country that had broken free of Vanisher rule. They dated from the breaking of the world, and were infused with an odd, drunken enthusiasm, the writer heady on the promise of freedom from Vanishers: odd, disjointed readings about a future that hadn't come to pass.

"You're too serious," Vu Côn said, fondly. They had

their heart set on following in her footsteps and running the palace.

"You think I'm a child." Thông's voice was mildly frustrated. They were growing up too fast, too uncontrollably. And so was Liên. Vu Côn thought of Hoang again, and wondered how things would have gone, had he been alive.

"I don't," Vu Côn said. "But there are some things you're not ready for." The vast, dangerous world, the one that would dazzle and cut them at the same time.

Thông said, finally, "You gave her the run of the palace. You've not done that for any of the others."

"The other patients?" Vu Côn asked, finally. The hundred, the thousands in the cradle-rooms, who had come beseeching her and who now awaited healing or death or both. "She's not infected. Or dangerous." But, as she said that, she remembered Yên, coming to stand in her path as she left with the healer in her arms—facing her, shaking with fear—remembered that odd thrill going through her, almost a mirror of the fear in Yên's face. It was nonsense. She was a dragon. Even had Yên been the most skilled of scholar-magicians, Vu Côn's powers would have dwarfed hers. But, in that moment, Vu Côn had had the feeling of facing an unbreakable wall, that not even grievous wounds or death would stop Yên from barring her way.

"Filial piety," Vu Côn said, slowly, carefully. She'd almost forgotten what the word actually meant. "I suppose she's here because she impressed me."

Thông laughed. They were still tense, but it had abated.

"What?" Vu Côn asked.

"You've been alone for too long, Mother." They shook their head. "A mortal, of all things."

Vu Côn bristled. "We're not sleeping together."

"Because she'd say no? You know she wouldn't. I've seen her making puppy eyes at you."

Because she'd seen the horror in Yên's eyes when she'd made an angry, ill-timed jab about warm bodies in her bed. Vu Côn breathed out. "We've discussed this before. Not just other people saying yes, but whether they mean it, or whether they're just doing it because they're afraid." They didn't quite get that, she knew: neither them nor Liên. Was it genetic, something even years and years of nurturing hadn't managed to eradicate?

Thông sighed. Words hung in the air for a moment as they did so: the blurred, silver traceries of a language that could change the world. "Duty is easier than grief."

"I said that," Vu Côn said. She didn't smile, because the memories that came with that were painful. Tuyêt, who'd always smiled even under Vanisher rule, still with that same smile as they buried the wives they'd lost in the breaking of the world—their mane of hair streaming in the wind, their fangs glinting in the darkness. Hanh Vang, with the turtles' scales on her eyes and wrists and fingernails, standing very straight, dripping the sheening, oily water of polluted lakes and repeating that it would all be fine. Du Khach, halfway between rooster and woman, clinging to her maps as if they could make sense of the world—the vast spreads of emptiness on them with only the occasional city dotted across the forbidding landscape.

After a while, all they'd seen when looking at each other was unbearable loss. It'd been easier, then, to just— not go, but drift apart. To retreat: all the spirits that had once protected the land, shutting themselves in their own fortresses. Vu Côn hadn't. She'd remained in the world to answer prayers, to answer wishes, to safeguard what she could.

"All grief ends," Thông said, finally.

"You still want me to sleep with her."

Thông shrugged. "I'm supposed to want what's best for you. It doesn't mean you get a say in it."

"I think you'll find it will. If you read the First Teacher properly."

"Hmf," Thông said. "She could be a friend, then, Mother. You don't have to be so lonely."

Unlikely. No friendship under unequal terms, but she was used to solitude. "I can handle a lone mortal." And, after a pause: "Let's talk less about Yên and more about you."

Thông said, finally, "I don't want to worry you." They exhaled. Blurred silver words hung in the air in front of their snout.

As if that made her worry less. "I'm your mother,' Vu Côn said. "I'll always worry. Is there anything in particular I need to be more worried about?"

Another sigh. The words from this one hung in the air longer, no longer out of focus or illegible. These were sharp. These were words the palace would respond to. Vu Côn knew, then, with absolute certainty, what Thông was going to say. Fear took hold of her heart and squeezed. She forced herself to remain calm, to say nothing, because they needed to be the one saying it.

"I've woken up," Thông said. "Nightmares, except that my bed's been dismantled when I wake up. As if I'd been giving orders to the palace. Liên says"—they took a deep, shaking breath—"Liên says I talk in my sleep."

"It's nightmares," Vu Côn said, finally. "It doesn't mean you're losing control."

"Genetics," Thông said. "Some of your lessons did stick. I do know some things are hereditary."

"Like cruelty and thirst for power?" Vu Côn said. "That's rather a stretch."

"You don't understand," Thông said, low and intense. "They broke the world."

"Your genitors?" Vu Côn had taught herself, a long time ago, never to say "parent". Neither Thông nor Liên were hers by blood, but that wasn't what mattered. It shouldn't have. Except . . . except that, as Thông said, genetics were funny things. "They're gone now. Into their gates and ships and away from the world. They won't be coming back." They'd scorched and poisoned the earth, enslaved spirits and men, and finally moved on. And if it meant abandoning two of their own children . . . Obviously they hadn't cared, and wouldn't care enough to return.

Thông lifted a hand, stared at it. Scales flickered into existence on their skin, opalescent and fugitive, changing shapes as Vu Côn watched. "Won't they?" they asked. "You always say parents live on in their children."

"Parents," Vu Côn said, more forcefully than she meant to. Hearing them saying it had removed her fear. It wasn't real. It was more of children's nightmares and fancies, something it was her job to dispel. She'd sat with Thông and Liên when they were still very little—when they didn't know when to control their form and would become miniature versions of the beings who'd once been her masters, going through shape after shape in an effort to outrace the dark. It had been impossible, even with the physical resemblance, to see the small, shivering children on the bed as a threat. "Not genitors. The people who raise you. There is a difference."

"We killed Father," Thông said, finally.

"You did not," Vu Côn said. It was reflex. "It was his choice." Hoang had been the one who'd heard the cries, years before. He'd ventured into a ruined Vanisher hatchery, and found two screaming children in their cribs, still dripping from the fluids that had held them in stasis. He'd been herding them back to Vu Côn, back to safety, and less careful than he should have been against the palace defenses. The hatchery had seen only a servant trying to steal away babies, and sheared him in two as he reached the door, long before Vu Côn could find the control panel to stop it. She saw it, sometimes, in her nightmares; she heard the lament of his ghost, even though it was fanciful, self-indulgent imaginings.

Even dying, he hadn't regretted saving the twins, and neither had Vu Côn. She'd raised them as her own, and as they reached adolescence and adulthood, she was only starting to measure the magnitude of what she'd done.

They were *children*, her children, but the world hadn't changed that much since the breaking, and so many things in it remembered the Vanishers. She couldn't keep them safe forever, and she wasn't even sure she could keep them safe from themselves. But she had to try.

"Puberty is . . . fraught," Vu Côn said. She didn't know enough about the Vanisher equivalent. She could see it happening in Thông, in the way they'd shot up, their face losing the baby fat, their reptilian shape sprouting spikes and harder scales. She had no idea how much of this was normal. But it didn't matter. "Most species have hormones flooding their bodies. It makes for vivid dreams. That's all there is to it."

"It can't be that," Thông said.

Vu Côn smiled in a way she hoped was reassuring and firm. "Because you'd want to lose control?"

"No!"

"Look. It's normal to worry. I'd be more concerned if you didn't. There's . . . baggage," she said, carefully. "Medical history."

"Medical." Thông's voice was neutral, carefully so.

"You know as well as I do that some patients have more to overcome. It doesn't make it more or less likely to happen." Vu Côn said.

Thông's expression was distant: the healer's, again, dissecting probabilities and evidence. Liên was all emotions, but they were different. They said, finally, "I don't know. Maybe you're right. And maybe . . ." They were too well bred to contradict her openly.

"If I'm wrong," Vu Côn said, "we'll deal with those consequences, too. People don't suddenly snap. There's warning signs, and I'm not seeing them." Not beyond one over-worried, overwrought child with too much on their mind. "Why don't you just find something to read? Or some lessons to review?"

Thông snorted. "I'm not Liên."

"You asked about Yên," Vu Côn said, finally. "She's here to teach you. Duty. Behavior. Proper etiquette."

"You could have done that," Thông said.

"Yes," Vu Côn said. "I have." But in that, she knew she'd failed. The rules of the First Teacher didn't matter to her as much as they mattered to a scholar, and the twins had picked up on that from an early age. "You need to hear it from someone else." Yên was all fire and belief. She thought, again, of her standing to prevent Vu Côn from leaving the house. All passion, and hopefully the twins would respond to some of that. "Do you think I never lose control? All those rules, all those maxims: they're how we remember. How we put on the mask of civilization over our baser instincts."

Thông watched her, for a while. Then they snorted again. "It's a good excuse," they said. "For having her around."

Vu Côn shook her head. "Do stop," she said, keeping her voice low and pleasant. She was *not* attracted to Yên. Or, more accurately: she was attracted, but she knew the cost of giving in.

She had it all under control.

* * *

Days passed, and it became hard to remember the village. Shrieking, dusty children in a small and cramped classroom, and Mother's voice, and the smell of fish sauce and garlic on hands, all of it faded to dusty nothingness. All of it felt like a dream, every morning when Yên woke up inside the room with the walls stretching away from her into vertiginous infinity. At night, she dreamt that she hadn't been saved: that everything led, as she'd always known it would, to the purifying circle—to its cold, merciless light, that single suspended moment before it flayed her, skin and muscle and bone . . . And then she'd wake up, gasping, trying to breathe, raising her hands to her face, remembering Vu Côn's touch on her skin, as wet and as cold as the oily river.

She'd tried to go out, several times. To find a way back out the river or wherever Vu Côn really lived, but there was nothing. Corridors twisting and stretching, windows opening onto impossible landscapes, towers upside down, fountains and basins that fed back into themselves. The palace might not have been designed as a prison, but there was no way out. And, every time she opened a door, she thought of Vu Côn's warnings. Viruses. Diseases. How would she know, if she was contaminated? Was there even any truth in that, or was it a way for Vu Côn to keep her penned in the palace?

Every night, the same prayers to her ancestors, asking them to watch over Mother, asking Elder Giang to watch over Mother, because she was desperate and could think of no one else she could beseech.

Vu Côn left her alone, which was equal parts good and frustrating. In some ways, Yên didn't want to think about her, about that strange, unhealthy thrill of looking into the dragon's eyes, the rush of desire that had made the world contract when Vu Côn had touched her. But in others . . . she wanted to argue with Vu Côn. To tell her she *wasn't* getting used to being there, that she missed Mother and Oanh and the village—that she even missed Elder Giang, which was something.

One morning, Yên made her way to the vast, deserted rooms of the kitchen to find the twins there. It wasn't an uncommon occurrence: the palace seemed to have no inhabitants other than the twins and Vu Côn, but every morning Yên would find steaming hot breakfast on a table, a bewildering array of odd-tasting foods, of soups that were too sharp, noodles that were too soft, buns too white and too smooth to seem real. The flour of legends, without blackness or insects or grit.

The uncommon thing was that neither Thông nor Liên appeared to be eating. They were simply waiting for her: Liên in a simple set of fluid robes that moved like water, and Thông wearing the robes of an official, not the embroidered wealth Yên had seen on traveling scholar-magicians from the cities, but a simple, deceptively deep scarlet that never quite remained the same color, shifting as the light caught it.

Yên could have asked if she was late, but she'd never get an answer: neither of the twins would ever accuse their own respected teacher. Besides, she was famished, and food, no matter how odd-tasting, shouldn't be wasted. She headed to the metal table, thanking the ancestors and all the spirits that the kitchen was one of the only rooms where geometry seemed to behave normally, with only a few engravings of dragons growing larger and larger on the ceiling—the endmost scales on the larger dragons turning out to be the seed of small dragons going into the other direction. Bewildering, but not dizzying.

"Grab some food," Thông said. "We're going to the library today."

Yên paused, halfway to an oddly puffed-up fritter. She couldn't help it. It was like holding rice to a famished man, or sleep to an exhausted one. "There's a library here?"

"Of course!" Liên said. She smiled, a toothy, white smile that Yên suddenly saw as dazzling instead of frightening.

"She's been worrying at Mother for days, trying to get permission," Thông said. They hid an obvious smile of fondness.

"Like you haven't been doing the same thing." Liên crossed her arms over her chest.

"I don't boast," Thông said, almost gently.

"I don't understand," Yên said. "Your mother—Vu Côn gave me permission to go wherever I want in the palace."

Liên nodded. "The library is hidden," she said. "And locked."

Like the doors to the outside world Yên couldn't find in the labyrinth of corridors and upside-down gardens? "Why?"

"Because it's dangerous. The words in the books are magic," Liên started, but Thông held up a hand.

"That's not what she's asking," they said. And, with a sigh: "Because you're unhappy."

Yên stared at them. Wherever she'd thought mercy and compassion would come from, she hadn't thought it'd be her students. Her unruly, rowdy students who seemed to be sitting down with her out of boredom and duty to their mother, rather than interest—always chafing, in a hurry to leave and do something that didn't involve discussing the First Teacher's maxims. "I'm—" She opened her mouth to say that she was not, and then closed it.

She could have asked how they knew, but she was sure she wouldn't like the answer.

"Fine." Yên went back to the table and picked up a bowl of noodle soup, breathing the familiar smell of star anise. She wasn't sure by what miracle it remained hot. When asked, Thông would raise their eyebrows and say, "Things working as they should," and Liên wasn't much more helpful. "Is it far away?"

Thông shrugged. "Not much."

"There's a tricky corridor, though," Liên said. "We got stuck there once."

"Younger sis!" Thông frowned, again. "Don't scare her."

"We were much younger," Liên said. She spoke a word in an alien language, and luminous words hung in the air for a bare moment. Was it the language of the spirits? Yên hadn't dared ask, though it wasn't the first time the twins had spoken it. "Now we've got the palace sorted out." Liên looked as though she was going to say more, but Thông cut her off.

"Are you ready?"

Yên finished chewing her fritter, and followed them. The greasy dough sat uncomfortably in her stomach as they walked through the palace corridors, going past vertiginous room after room. She got, once more, the impression that she was going to throw up.

They didn't go to the courtyard where she usually taught the twins: instead, Thông took a corridor that flared out, becoming windows on either side of them, with a distant, hazy landscape Yên couldn't quite make out.

"Don't look down," Thông said, casually, as they rounded a corner and the windows became more ornate: sculpted, filigreed metals with cascades of light giving the frames different colors. In each was the same landscape, over and over—not just the same place, but the same features: a set of rocky spurs with a temple clinging to their summit, a dozen scattered buildings with corroded metal roofs, shining in the light of a sun and an overlarge moon. No, not quite the same: in each window, the sun and moon were in slightly different configurations, from dawn to noon to dusk, the moon hanging from low to high over the horizon.

Yên tried to keep her eyes on the windows. But the corridor flared out and stopped twisting and turning, and she lost the fight. The floor she was on . . . There was no floor, merely more windows, except with two suns instead of a sun and a moon—and the very slight yield she'd felt, which she'd taken as her walking on different tiles of a floor, was in fact the windows, flexing slightly as she stepped on them—not like glass but like a pane of water stretched so taut it wouldn't break . . . .

Thông's arm on her steadied her. "I told you not to look down."

"We're almost there," Liên said. "Hang on."

"Here." Between two of the windows—if one could keep their gaze on the windows without nausea—was a slight space, just large enough for one person to squeeze in. It barely merited the name of *door*. Liên laid her hand on the panel, unperturbed by the window on her left, where the sky above the building was ablaze with glowing lava, the moon and the sun themselves falling to ashes in large blackened chunks. Words lit up slowly and lazily: they were the same script as Vu Côn's robe. Something clicked. Liên pushed, and the wall disappeared, as if the floor had swallowed it up. A thin sliver of light replaced it.

Thông stopped Yên as she was about to go in. "Us first," they said.

"I thought it was safe."

Thông snorted. "The Vanishers broke the world and left. Do you expect their dwellings to be safe?

Liên slid in. As she did so, her arms turned into scaled claws for a fraction of a second, leaving gouges in the door frame. After a moment, her voice came floating out of the darkness: "All good," she said.

Yên squeezed in. It was a tight fit, and she understood now why Liên had struggled. Yên was thinner: turning sideways, she could just fit into the door. She could feel Thông's breath, slow and even, at her back, and then she was through, and blinded with light.

"Oh."

The library stretched over and around her: a sphere of light and steel, a sweeping, shimmering room like the sky at dawn, when everything was still grey but a faint reddish tinge colored the thick layer of pollution clouds. It didn't have shelves, but rather row after row of pillars, labelled with that same alphabet she couldn't read, going on and on and up, clinging to the walls as though gravity didn't matter. Each of them was faceted and a different color, like huge jewels scattered inside a sphere so big, Yên could barely comprehend its dimensions.

Liên was standing at the nearest one, which was the green of jade and freshly cut grass, faintly opalescent and shimmering with an inner light that showed up the veins and imperfections in sharp contrast. "Long Châu's *The Moon's Path*." The words flowed out of her mouth, transfigured into letters. She hadn't had to write them, as a scholar-magician would have done. They simply appeared, clinging to the air like a flock of butterflies. The pillar shivered and contracted, the letters within flowing faster for a fraction of a second. Then a book appeared from a slot halfway up the pillar. Flecks of light clung to it like dust. Liên waved it at Yên. "Want to try?"

Yên let out a breath she hadn't been aware of holding.

The Vanishers had broken and poisoned the world; she'd had no idea that they could create such breathtaking beauty. "Yes," she said.

Up close, the pillar was nothing like stone, more like polished metal given a slightly different sheen. Odd rectangular patterns were carved within it, parallel lines splitting around darker islands of pooled silver, converging toward squat nexuses in haphazard fashion. It looked like a child's drawing, random lines and circles, but nevertheless it didn't feel random, more like something that had its own logic. Yên laid a hand on the pillar. Something gripped her, a fist of ice closing around her wrist. Her hand up to her wrist was now the blue of the stone. Liên laughed. "It's normal. Go on, ask."

"I don't know any of the books there."

"Then just ask a normal question. It doesn't need to be a title."

Yên said, before she could think, "I want to know about magic."

The pillar went deathly still, the hand that was holding her as cold as a corpse. A faint, faint heartbeat, a memory of something living, slowly rose, reverberating through the pillar. Words floated on its surface: a single one detached itself and hovered at her height, steadily blinking. It wasn't a word Yên knew, but as she watched it shifted to something else, an older, distorted version of "speech".

"Magic is speech?" she asked.

Liên shrugged. "Everything answers to speech here."

"I was hoping—" Yên stopped because she didn't know what she was hoping for. She'd tried studying magic, the words Mother painstakingly calligraphied around her patients' beds to cast the healing spell, but to her they were nothing but abstract terms. She could guess where they'd come from and where they'd slot into a disser-tation, but they never came alive for her as they did for Mother, never healed someone or moved things or started fires. She'd thought she'd made her peace with not know-ing them—not every scholar needed to be a scholar-magi-cian—but being in the palace and unable to make things work had sharpened her hunger for understanding.

She reached with her free hand, touched the single word. The pillar shook again and spat out a book, just as the hold on her hand vanished.

The text on it was the same archaic language as Vu Côn's dress. When she opened it, she saw words in the same alphabet, except that the alignment seemed all wrong. The words felt too clumped together, too dense, compared to the ones she'd already seen.

"That's a primer on Vanisher magic," Thông said, behind her. "Small, petty spells: it was for their servants' use."

Vanisher magic? The book tumbled out of Yên's hands before she could think.

Liên laughed. "It's not contagious!"

The Vanishers had broken the world. They had taken and enslaved as they'd wished, leaving constructs and plagues as their legacies. Their magic was all chains and knives and diseases, everything that bound and broke and devastated. Even their rare healings had been double-edged, leaving people riddled with tumors and shriveled elements.

"I—" Yên swallowed. "Maybe something else."

Liên shrugged. She touched the pillar again, said something in dragon language. A book coalesced into the slot. "Here," she said.

It looked old. It couldn't be old, because surely the library—the pillar—had made it at Liên's request. But the pages were crinkled and yellow, the binding repaired in several places. The title, even in distorted archaic, was intimately familiar. "*Commentary on the Fourth Teaching.*" She breathed slowly, evenly. She'd known there was an original to this book, that it hadn't been written in Việt but transcribed afterward. She'd known that everything they had was bad, distorted copies.

She had no idea that she'd one day be holding a perfect one.

The Broken-World Teacher's words: everything their disciples had collected after the Vanishers tore them to pieces for their presumption, all the maxims and the proverbs and the poems, the painstaking work that had eventually led to all the scholar-magicians, their own defense against the darkness.

She breathed out, again. The book still hadn't vanished. "I can keep it?" she asked.

Thông laughed. It was a rare and precious sound, unburdened by their usual seriousness. "It'll make other copies if anyone asks."

"There used to be limits on how much we could borrow at the same time," Liên said. By her tone, it sounded like they'd thoroughly tested them. "But we fixed that."

"Excluding the brief interval where everything that came out of here crumbled as soon as you moved a finger."

Liên snorted. "Design flaw. We figured out the right words, didn't we?"

Yên sought words, carefully. "You're very fluent with the technology."

Liên laughed. Thông's laughter, this time, was barbed. "You have to be," Thông said. "It's that or go mad with boredom."

They sounded . . . angry, as if Yên had touched on a sore spot. And no wonder. Had the twins been prisoners there all their childhood?

Thông must have seen Yên's face.

"We're not prisoners." They laughed, as if mildly annoyed with themself. "Would you trust Liên, out in the world? She'd get herself killed."

Liên made that frustrated snorting sound again. "Mother treats us like we're celadon and might break at any moment."

Thông said nothing. Neither did Yên. She'd seen that odd mixture of maturity and childishness before, in teenagers forced to grow up too fast. "Your father—" she said, finally.

"Dead," Thông said. The word was final, like a grave snapping shut.

"I'm sorry." Yên said.

Aliette de Bodard

"Don't be."

Yên clutched the book, looked, again, at the library. How much knowledge was there in the scattered pillars? What were they used for; why were they all different? But instead, looking at Thông, at the way they held themself—marking time, Yên knew suddenly, with absolute certainty, because she'd seen it in dozens of her students back in the village—she found another question bubbling up. "Why are we here?" she asked. "Really."

"You're unhappy," Thông said, glibly and easily. Too distracted to put too much effort in their pretense.

"No," Yên said. "Not that. Did Vu Côn—" Why would Vu Côn ask anything of them? It made no sense.

"We do have our own initiative," Liên said, mildly.

"You do," Yên said. She pointed to Thông. "You're counting. Marking the passage of time. Something is happening in the palace, isn't it? Something I shouldn't be seeing?" And what better distraction for a scholar than a library?

At length Liên said, "It's not safe to be in our classroom today, Teacher."

"Less safe than usual?" In ordinary times, Yên would have made a better effort, but she was tired.

"You've noticed Mother is out most of the time," Thông said.

Which explained why Vu Côn hadn't talked to her since the first day. "Answering summons?"

"Traveling. Making sure the world doesn't break further. It carries its own risks. Traveling isn't exactly safe nowadays," Thông said, curtly.

62

"She's busy," Liên said. There was a hint of bitterness in her voice. "She's thrown herself into her work since . . ." She paused, started again. "Duty comes before anything else, for her."

Yên said, "I'm not sure what that duty is."

"What the Vanishers bequeathed her." Liên laughed but there was still no joy in her face. "All the mess of the broken world. And us, of course, on top of that."

The twins were a handful, to be sure, but no more and no less than other teenagers their age. "The joys of motherhood," Yên said, keeping her face straight. "You're not answering my question."

"It's audience day."

Which meant nothing to Yên.

"People come to see Mother and beseech her for favors. *They're* not safe."

Yên struggled to reconcile this with the palace. "There is no one here." There were no exits, no easy way of getting out.

"You can get here from the outside world," Thông said. "If you're motivated enough."

"Heart's desire," Liên said. "Like your mother did, when she summoned Mother."

A reference to Mother on a dragon's lips didn't head the list of welcome subjects for Yên.

"Getting out is another matter," Thông said. They sounded darkly amused. Their hands played with something Yên couldn't see, which emitted small, regular sparks of icy blue light.

"Because your mother takes random prisoners?" It was cheap and easy. Yên knew Thông would likely let it pass, out of respect for their teacher.

"Because you can't tell what you get, when you ask for favors."

Something small and hard was coalescing in Yên's belly—a cold fury she'd sat on for too long, hearing Thông and Liên speaking about twisting and taking lives as though it meant nothing—not making excuses for Vu Côn, but treating it all as though it was perfectly natural. They were children, of course. They couldn't know—

But within her were the old, old words, the merciless ones that had guided scholars since times immemorial, as sharp and as brilliant as naked blades.

The virtuous person examines their heart, that there may be nothing wrong there . . . .

If you see what is right and fail to act on it, you lack courage.

Liên and Thong were still talking, sounding distant and tinny. "They mostly beseech Mother for cures, in any case," Liên was saying. "As if we could do these anymore . . ."

Thông's gaze was stern. "We do what we can. And my earlier point remains. The risk of contagion . . ."

Mother had done what she could, too, which was, all too often, making patients comfortable while they died. Mother—

What kind of a filial daughter was Yên, to let herself be cowed into inactivity? "I want to see her," Yên said.

Shocked silence. Then a scrabble, as Thông stumbled against the pillar they were leaning against. Their body was shifting, lengthening. Subtle traceries of light hung behind them, a wealth of words in that alphabet Yên couldn't read. "Respectfully—"

"You said people came to see her. To beseech her. Anyone can do this?"

"Yes," Thông said. They looked uncomfortable, trying to figure out how much they dared to reproach Yên. Courage won out. Yên felt for them, but she couldn't allow that to sway her. "Respectfully, Teacher, that's a bad idea."

Worse than being stuck in the palace, coddled like a child? "I think not," Yên said, as coldly as she could muster. Vu Côn may have owned her life, but that didn't mean she got to dictate every waking hour of it.

4

The Watcher in the Dark

When Yên came into the audience chamber, the first thing she saw was the body.

It was lying off to the side, by the walls—the part of them that didn't stretch away to infinity—looking small and pathetic, its throat raggedly torn out. Blood, pooling out in odd, haphazard splashes, though there was very little of it. Old memories and instincts took over, from working with Mother's patients. She knelt and touched the wrist, looking for the pulses of the heart threaded throughout the body. Nothing. They must have been dead before the throat-tearing. Not that it made it any better.

Thông whispered something under their breath. Minute, silver words left their mouth, clinging to Yên's hands. Yên's skin started to itch and burn. She snatched her hand back from the body, and the pressure eased.

"Teacher, please," Thông said. "Do you remember what I said?"

Contagion. "They got their throat torn out," Yên pointed out. There'd been no pulse.

"Too little blood. They didn't die of the torn throat. And some viruses travel in the blood. Most of them very, very nasty." At length, in a different voice: "I'm sorry for showing disrespect."

"It's all right." Yên had played fast and loose with it herself.

"Audience" made the entire thing seem far larger than it was: there were only a handful of people ahead of Yên. They seemed infinitely far away, standing with a particular glaze in their eyes, as if they were dreaming awake. They weren't talking to each other. One was coughing, a particularly nasty thing that racked their entire body, rising to a peculiar pitch, like the trill of a bird. After each coughing fit, they would fall down on one knee, and get back up. One had sores over their entire body, and the one closest to Yên was carrying a shivering, pale child in his arms. The child was perhaps nine, ten years old, barely older than Vinh.

When they moved, Yên saw, for a second, a translucent shape moving under the skin of their face, darker-skinned and thinner, like the shadow of a corpse's skull. The âm self—the shadow-self, the moon self, except that it was completely shriveled away instead of being in balance with the duong self. Yên shivered. This far gone, there was no cure. Âm and duong—moon and sun, darkness and light, the fundamental duality that underpinned the universe—were meant to always be in perfect balance, always carrying the seed of each other within themselves. The child had perhaps two, three months left to live before they simply wasted away.

Because she had to, Yên looked up; and down again, quickly, before she could be overwhelmed. The room stretched and twisted. Rivulets of water ran down on either side of the path leading to the throne where Vu Côn sat, gradually gathering to become a huge river that climbed over the throne and then fell back behind it, a soundless, impossible waterfall. But the rivulets went on and on, receding into the distance and forming another, farther-away waterfall falling on an empty throne, and on and on, repeating without any sign that this pattern ever ended. The air was saturated with a clean, sharp, and unfamiliar smell, almost like the smell of the monsoon, but strangely characterless: it didn't leave an oily after-taste in the mouth, or bring tears to Yên's eyes with its sharpness. *Clean*, she thought, and the word itself felt alien to her.

"This is a bad idea," Liên said.

"You don't have to come," Yên said.

Thông snorted. "As if."

Yên looked up again, tried to focus on Vu Côn. The dragon wore her hair in an ornate topknot, with jeweled pins that glinted in the semi-darkness of the room. Her tunic was layer after layer of purple clothes of slightly different hues, sheening to silver when she moved. None of the layers hid the shape of her strong, lithe body, or the presence Yên could feel, pressing against her even from the back of the room. Yên's heart was beating faster, a symphony of panic and desire conjoined in her throat.

The person with the child in their arms had reached

Vu Côn when she looked up and saw Yên, who was still carrying the book from the library, clutching it to her chest, a pathetic, ineffectual shield.

Vu Côn's face went still, as if time had stopped. Her eyes were two pools of darkness in the brown oval of her face, depths into which burnt the cold, cold ice of the sea's depths—catching Yên's gaze and drowning her, over and over. "You," she said. Her voice carried perfectly to the end of the room.

Yên knelt, the full obedience reserved for an empress in a distant city she would likely never see: forehead on the floor, feeling the coolness of water on her brow. "I beseech you," she said, in the growing silence.

Nothing, for a while. Whispers she couldn't make out. Thông and Liên walking out from behind her, their feet getting closer to the throne. An animated conversation that Yên caught only fragments of, Vu Côn's voice the thunder of killing water.

At length, after what felt like an eternity: "Come here," Vu Côn said.

The child and their parent were standing beside the throne: outlined for a bare moment in a radiance made of thousands of words before they faded away, an afterimage swiftly banished. As if they'd never been there at all. Had they come back to the outside world? Had they—

Enough. She couldn't afford to think of any of this.

There were two other bodies at Vu Côn's feet, with no visible wounds: only a thin, watered-down dot of blood on their rough-spun tunics.

Yên stood at the foot of the steps, not meeting Vu Côn's eyes for fear of disrespect. "Up here," Vu Côn said. Her voice was still mild. Thông and Liên had fanned out on either side of her. They were both silent, looking distinctly chastened, and fully human. Maintaining that shape was obviously taking a toll on Liên, who kept shivering, staring at the door out of the room with longing.

Yên was going to get killed. Or punished in some other way. She never should have—

Up close, Vu Côn's presence was even more unbearable. She stood a handspan away from Yên. Close enough to touch, close enough to kiss. "Well?" she asked.

Yên swallowed, forced herself to speak. No choice, not anymore. "You go out into the world."

"Of course."

"Will you consider taking a message to my mother?"

A silence. Yên didn't mistake it for acquiescence. "Please. She's all I have, and she thinks I'm dead. If I could let her know—"

"That you're not dead?" Yên kept expecting Vu Côn to touch her. She'd been steeling herself against it, reproaching herself for wanting it. But the dragon hadn't moved. "I told you. You might as well be."

"But I'm not!" Yên let anger out, briefly. It was the only way she'd ever feel brave enough to argue with a spirit who held her life in their hands. "I understand you don't want me to see her. That"—she swallowed—"the village would not take me back in." That it was true didn't make it any less hurtful. "But surely—"

"Surely, she should know that you're in a spirit world, unable to ever come back? You think that would be some comfort?"

"Yes," Yên said. "Because I'm alive. Because there's hope."

A hope that, if she listened to the twins, Vu Côn had lost a long time before. Another silence. At length, Vu Côn said, "You dare much." *Too much*, her voice said.

The world, Mother said quietly in Yên's mind, *is unfair*. A little fairer now, with the Vanishers gone. But also broken and twisted out of shape, struggling to recover from a hundred thousand strictures imposed on it.

Yên lifted her head, still not looking at Vu Côn. It'd be so easy for the dragon to kill her, arguing disrespect. Yên didn't even understand half the rules, nor did she expect to. Who knew what laws bound spirits, especially in the world after the breaking? "Then just kill me. At least it'd be cleaner."

To Yên's surprise, Thông spoke up. "She's been distracted. Weeping in her room, when she thinks we can't see her." And, to Yên: "I'm sorry, Teacher."

"And you think this is going to make me be in a better mood?" Vu Côn sighed. "What did I tell you about respect for teachers?"

Thông's voice was soft. "It's what she wants. Against that—"

"The cost of revealing this matters little? That's . . . some rather creative interpretation of filial respect." Vu Côn didn't sound altogether happy.

"You were the one who told me," Thông said. "The old rules no longer apply. We need to change."

Another silence, but the anger had receded a fraction. "All things do." And, to Yên, more softly: "I'll take your message, should my duties get me back to your province."

Yên's lips shaped around a "thank you," but she was choking on it. Why should she thank Vu Côn for basic pity and courtesy? "It's good of you," she said, finally.

Vu Côn raised an eyebrow.

Thông looked as though they were going to kick Yên for failing to be properly respectful. Yên swallowed, tried again. What had happened to her scholar's smooth, honeyed tongue? But she knew she'd never had one. "I appreciate it," she said. "Very much."

A silence. Then: "Honest, if nothing else."

"You knew this," Liên said.

"Sincerity being the mark of the gentleperson scholar? Very well." Vu Côn shook her head. Her face shifted, became the dragon's, with the shadow of antlers crowning her face, and a long, thin moustache falling on either side of a thin, curved mouth filled with fangs. "Was there anything else?" She gestured, with lengthening sleeves, to the people still waiting in the audience room. "I have work."

Yên looked, again, at the bodies strewn at the foot of the dais. The one farther away in the audience room had started to fade away, like the parent and their child but slower, the outline becoming more and more indistinct as the words that surrounded it became more and more pronounced. Why had they died? She could ask, but she knew she'd reached the ends of Vu Côn's patience. The dragon was not distantly amused as she'd been in the Plague Grove, but taut and angry. Was it because Yên had defied her? Or because she'd brought the children into it—not, of course, that the twins had done anything but bring themselves.

Liên tugged at her sleeve. She was shaking now, the outline of scales flashing under her skin, her face taut with effort. "Come on, Teacher. You can write your letter? While we read *The Pale Turtle's Sword.*"

Yên went down the steps in silence. As she withdrew from the room, just a few steps from the pale imprint of the corpse, she turned, and met Vu Côn's eyes. The dragon's eyes were a light grey, the color of storm clouds gathering. She was looking straight at Yên with an expression that was half-irritation, half-hunger, as if she would gobble Yên whole, given half a chance.

And what scared Yên most? This might, in the end, be just what she longed for.

* * *

Yên woke up in a dark, silent room. Her belly was clenched with fear, her muscles all stiff, as if she'd run and run during her sleep. She could only remember vague strands of a nightmare: Mother dead, Vu Côn chasing her through a forest of trees crumbling into ashes, the scales of her draconic body shimmering through the holes left by the burnt tree, burning, burning so bright they drowned out everything . . . .

A dream. It was just a dream. She'd go back to sleep and it would all be fine. It—

There was someone in the room, watching her.

She didn't know how, or why. Just this cold, hard certainty, a fist of ice tightening around her guts. The impossible perspective was illuminated with a faint blue light, the same way it always was, but now it felt like instead of leading into some other, faraway world, it opened on somewhere very close—somewhere the Vanishers waited, watching, for anyone foolish enough to trespass on what was theirs.

Malice.

There was something, in the depths of the light. A blurred shape. A person. Not a human one: claws and too-long arms, and a crest rising from the back of their neck, climbing to where their hair should have been.

If Yên moved, if she breathed, they would see her. They would—she'd heard all the stories. They would take her apart, hurt and hunt her for fun. If—

Her breath burnt in her lungs. She couldn't move. She didn't dare move. But, if she didn't, they'd catch her anyway.

She needed to do something.

The book she'd taken from the library glowed on the bedside table. Her hands, moving agonizingly slowly, moved through a familiar sequence: the Broken-World Teacher's most basic mantra, the one for protection against evil spirits. *Spiral. Turtle's Claw. Crossbow. Fortress.* Again and again, and nothing happening. No glowing signs, no sense of power. She wasn't meant for magic: it was a talent, and she didn't have it. She'd known this. She hadn't taken the book hoping to wield its power, but simply to understand. To take it all apart as she took apart ancient texts in her classroom.

But, as her hands moved, again and again, shaping the old words of power, the knot of fear in her stomach eased, and her breath no longer burnt in her throat. *Spiral. Turtle's Claw. Crossbow. Fortress.* She was in that timeless, fearless place where she didn't have to think about anything making sense or frightening her. There were only the words, and the way they fitted together. The strokes on "spiral" that formed the first glimmers of the fortress's wall, echoed by the sharp turn of "claw," a reminder of weapons, of impregnability dearly bought.

Spiral. Turtle's Claw. Crossbow. Fortress.

She rose, heedless of the dark shadow in the room, and ran toward the door. In her mind were only the words. The two turns in the writing for "crossbow," the way the string was tightened, broken in the middle, along the frame of the crossbow; and the turtle, in the center of it all, the spirit that had always protected the land and its rivers and sea.

When she stopped on the threshold, pausing for breath, the shadow was standing by her bedside, reaching down.

She ran.

It was night in the palace, and nothing made sense anymore: courtyards with towers that became underground silos, gardens with trees on every wall and roof, endless rooms where the windows opened on a hundred, a thousand different realities, where two suns became a sun eaten by a wolf became ten crows of fire spreading burning winds amidst a hail of arrows, where the moon was encircled by the roots of a banyan tree, its leaves falling pale and lifeless over the ruins of the earth . . . .

"Yên?"

It was Vu Côn. The dragon was wearing a dressing gown with embroidered peaches, billowing in some unseen wind. She stood in the middle of a corridor, looking puzzled. "I was wondering what all the racket was."

Yên stopped. The words in her mind stopped too, their shape lit for a few seconds more in her thoughts—*spiral turtle's claw crossbow fortress*—and then slowly dying away, like embers deprived of air. As they did, she realized—another kind of cold, hard certainty clenching her chest—that she was wearing pyjamas, standing barefoot in a palace that wasn't hers, facing the being who had claimed her life.

"I'm sorry," she said, dully. "I'll—" She started saying she'd go back to her room, and then she thought of the shadow by her bed. "I'll not bother you anymore." She'd find somewhere else to sleep. A garden, a courtyard. Somewhere, anywhere she didn't have to face the walls in her room again.

Vu Côn looked at her, for a while. She cocked her head in a disturbingly lizard-like fashion. Scales glimmered on her cheeks. "You're in shock."

"It's nothing," Yên said.

Time froze, slowed down to a trickle. Vu Côn was pushing her, steering her through one more corridor that was all empty, vertiginous spaces. An open door, with letters in the spirits' alphabet, glimmering on the panels, and only darkness inside. She was sitting on something soft, staring at a huge painting of the Four Immortals of the North: the Golden Princess stood over the corpses of animals who'd died in an epidemic, surrounded by a tangle of pink ribbons like writhing snakes.

Soft. A bed. She was sitting on Vu Côn's bed.

If embarrassment had been bad before, it was now terminal. "There was someone in my room," Yên said, her cheeks flaming. Shock was receding. She just wanted to dive under the bed and never emerge. Or to run away before Vu Côn saw her. All useless fancies, as she'd be caught before she even lifted a hand or foot.

Warmth on her fingers. She was holding a cup of tea, which she didn't remember taking: a soft celadon eggshell one, the cracks an intricate design, a labyrinth in some unknown language. She took a sip. The tea was odd, not the comforting bitter aftertaste she'd been used to in the kitchens. It was soft, almost tasteless.

Vu Côn was leaning against one of the bedposts, watching her. "Better?" she asked. Her dressing gown was parted, showing her chest, her dark skin rippling with each breath. Yên closed her eyes.

Definitely not better.

She opened her eyes again, focused her gaze on the

floor: shining, polished metal, with carved grooves. She said, again, "There was someone in my room."

"I heard it the first time." Vu Côn sounded distantly amused.

Yên's cheeks flamed again. "I wasn't thinking," she said, finally. She hadn't repeated it for Vu Côn, but for herself, because the words helped steady her.

Vu Côn flowed from bed to door. She traced, carefully, words on the panels. Yên could almost read them, something about palaces and safety. They glowed a liquid blue against the paler metal of the door. "Wait here," she said. The scales on her cheeks were thicker, her body lengthening under the robes.

"But—" She was going to leave Yên alone while she went out to have a look. She couldn't. That room was just the same as Yên's room, just as susceptible to Vanisher interference.

Vu Côn paused. She turned. She was a dragon now, fangs protruding through her snout, eyes the color of storm clouds, and flew to Yên. Her hands—claws, skin as rough as sandpaper, cold and slimy and yet not altogether unpleasant—closed over Yên's own hands and the cup. "I have to check, before whatever you saw leaves," she said. "You've seen the signs on the door. This is the heart of my power. There is nothing, not even Vanishers at the height of their powers, that could breach these doors."

"The walls," Yên said, struggling to speak. The steam from the tea was trapped in their embrace, gently warming them up. Her fingers felt soft, impossibly relaxed. "It came through the walls."

Vu Côn's face didn't change. "Nothing could breach the walls of this bedroom, either." A pause, then: "I'm not sending the twins into danger, but I can wake them up, if it would help."

The words on the door glowed. They cast a shadow, a darkness shot through with their interlaced letters: the same shadows Yên had seen before in Oanh's home, trailing in Vu Côn's wake. Yên felt the coldness of Vu Côn's flesh on her hand. She'd been half-repulsed, half-attracted before. Now she hungered for that moment to never end. She couldn't bear the thought of the twins piling into the bedroom, making small chatter and dissecting everything and anything. "I'll be fine," she said.

Vu Côn gave her a sharp look. She looked as though she might argue, and really, there was no way Yên could argue back. But at least Vu Côn moved away. "As you wish."

Yên stopped herself from reaching toward her, as Vu Côn leapt into the air and flew through the doorway. The panels slammed shut behind her: the words glimmered, once, twice. Darkness and silence spread absolute across the room. She'd barely looked at it. She'd gotten a confused image of a vast space with furniture scattered across a polished metal floor. There was a large table and a few chairs, and the dark, squat shape of bookshelves; and a mirror that glinted in the darkness. All of it felt . . . off, the wrong shape, the wrong proportions. Not quite the furniture in her room: not Vanishers, but perhaps Vu Côn's personal preferences?

Yên sat on the bed, sipping at a tea that had gone cold, trying not to think about where she was or why. In the shadows on the floor, the words spooled and unspooled, endlessly morphing into one another, a slow, inexorable pattern like a lullaby that whispered that she was safe. It would be so easy to listen to it, to believe.

She hadn't got a good look at the person—if they were indeed a person—by her bed. Perhaps it was just her fevered imagination? But she'd seen them. She'd felt their gaze on her. She hadn't imagined this. She'd been tired and in the grip of her nightmare, but she hadn't run away for nothing.

The words blinked, slowly, steadily.

When she looked up again, Vu Côn was standing by the bed.

Yên hadn't heard her enter, or the doors open. Vu Côn wasn't in dragon shape anymore. She was wearing her dressing gown again, and a single jade disk hung at her throat, glistening in the darkness. She smelled of musky wetness, with a faint hint of lotus flowers.

"Did you—"

"There was no one," Vu Côn said. She frowned.

Yên's cheeks flamed. "You mean I must have dreamt it."

When she dared to look up, Vu Côn was looking at her, thoughtfully. "No," she said. "I wasn't saying that." She fingered the pendant at her neck. As she did so, its light shone on the walls of the room: an endless series of mazes within mazes, not expanding outward like in Yên's room but into smaller and smaller dimensions, every detail becoming the seed of another, more compact maze. The pendant's radiance expanded: a warm and soft light, almost like daylight but with a deeper, yellower undertone. Yên's head ached.

"I saw the book on your bedside table," Vu Côn said.

Yên snorted. "You're going to say something about my being a scholar, always."

"No." Vu Côn's voice was serious. "You summoned magic in that room."

Yên stared at her. "I can't do magic."

"Why?"

"Why? Because it's never worked for me, that's why! Mother can write down words in circles and heal people. I—" She took a deep, shaking breath. "I know how the words work. I know how they're put together. But it's all theory."

"There's nothing wrong with theory," Vu Côn said. "My husband—" She stared at the darkness for a while, a pause that Yên didn't dare break through word or breath. "—my husband was a good theoretician. The best."

"I'm sorry," Yên said, before she could think. Vu Côn wouldn't want her sympathy. But the words were out of her mouth before she could clamp her lips on them.

Vu Côn shook her head, as if to clear a persistent thought. "There was magic in that room."

"The Vanishers—"

"—don't do that sort of magic." Something was obviously worrying her. She walked to the table. In the light, Yên saw that it was polished metal, engraved with a delicate, curving pattern of tree branches laden with peaches and kumquats. She dipped her hand into the bowl, and letters flowed from the tip of her hand to the hollow, sinking into the metal until they seemed to have always been part of it. Vu Côn retrieved a glass from the bowl and brought it back to Yên.

"Here, drink this. It'll help."

It tasted bitter and sharp, faintly familiar, like one of Mother's medicines. Something for shock? Yên drained it, feeling it settle in the pit of her stomach. She still felt faintly nauseous.

"You're homesick," Vu Côn said. "Very badly homesick."

Because Vu Côn had taken her from her village. Because—Yên thought of Elder Tho again, and of all of them, marching her to the Plague Grove to barter her like cattle—nothing more useful than a life to be given into servitude. Their fault. Vu Côn's fault. She wasn't sure anymore, just angry. "It's not my fault."

"I don't mean that," Vu Côn said. "I just mean that . . ." She paused, and cocked her head again. Her snout glistened in the light, droplets of water catching the yellow and refracting it in a harsh rainbow of colors. "Desire bends the world," she said. "And you're reading a book about changing the rules by which things work. A . . . syllabary of power."

"That I can't use." The words tasted like ashes on Yên's mouth.

Vu Côn went on, as if she hadn't spoken. "You want to go home. Badly enough to open a gate. Except . . ." She hesitated. "Except that not all gates lead where you'd expect."

A gate. Yên thought, again, of the walls opening. Of the figure standing on the threshold, waiting for her. She'd wanted to escape the palace so badly. She'd wanted to go home and find Mother and tell her that everything was all right, to find her old life and her students, Mother's querulous patients, even Elder Giang's cold and cryptic sympathy. Except that the gate she'd seen—the shining, wavering threshold beyond which all geometry seemed to become the bewildering infinite—wasn't anything she'd ever want to go through.

"Vanishers," she said.

"I don't think so," Vu Côn said. "The Vanishers are gone so far away that they're beyond our recall." She sounded relieved, and who wouldn't be? "But they've left other, no-more-palatable creatures behind them. Their guards, their enforcers. The people they took and twisted into their powers."

Yên was going to feel sick again. "I don't—"

"You were studying the book," Vu Côn said. "It has effects. May I?" She gestured toward Yên's hand.

"Yes," Yên said, not knowing what she meant.

Vu Côn took her hand. Her touch was cool: something from the depths, rising to hug Yên, to keep her forever safe. Letters flowed again, from her onto Yên's skin. Something about banyan trees and citadels, and other words she couldn't read. She reached out before she could think, and one of the words shimmered and died under her touch.

"No," Vu Côn said, gently. She took Yên's hand and set it aside. The words flowed again. Yên felt something shift and compress within her, as if she was being held underwater, her lungs burning. "There," Vu Côn said.

"I don't understand," Yên said.

"It's protection," Vu Côn said. The words still shone on Yên's hand, in the web between the thumb and index finger, a distant illumination like a tattoo made in silver dust instead of light. "A ward, if you wish. Something to contain the magic within you until you master it enough." Keeping Yên locked into the palace. Yên wanted to say something sharp about the convenience of it all, but the memory of that shape bending over her bed killed all sarcasm. The sheer malice she'd felt then, that distant amusement that drew its source from tearing the wings off birds and watching fish choke on land . . .

Yên breathed out, again. She felt odd. Tight, as if she couldn't quite breathe or move right. "I'm not a magician." But. But, if she was one, if she could somehow use this, if she could come back to the elders and show them this, or even go to another village . . . She'd have a use. She'd be valued.

"Perhaps." Vu Côn's voice was amused. "Perhaps not."

"The thing." Yên said. She breathed slowly, evenly. "The creature that came through that door."

"It's gone." Vu Côn's hands still held hers, stubbornly refusing to move. Yên found she didn't mind. "It hadn't materialized far enough."

"I saw it." She swallowed. "It bent over my bed."

"A shadow of a shadow." Vu Côn's eyes were hard. "There was nothing that had any physical presence in your room."

Yên said, finally, "It's safe?" She couldn't quite believe it.

"I can come and sleep in your room if you'd like," Vu Côn said. And, with a raised eyebrow: "On the floor, obviously. I'm not that kind of person."

"I know you're not." Ought she be reassured, or disappointed? She couldn't tell anymore. "I'm sorry, but—"

"There's no shortage of rooms," Vu Côn said. She shrugged. "Have one next door if that makes you feel better." And, carelessly, almost absentmindedly: "You don't have to decide now."

Which was good, because she didn't know what she wanted, right now.

"Thank you."

When Yên looked up again, Vu Côn was standing, watching her. She was mostly human again, with only the darkness in her too-wide eyes reminding Yên that she was a dragon. "I owe you an apology," she said.

That wasn't what Yên had expected to hear. "I don't understand."

"I made light of your homesickness. I shouldn't have. It's no easy thing, to see your entire world overturned."

"It's nothing." Yên searched for words in the scorched desert of her mind, and found only the truth. Vu Côn was going to make some flippant remark about genuine gratitude, show that same distant amusement she'd always shown to Yên. But she didn't.

"You said it was nothing. You're wrong. It was needlessly hurtful from me," Vu Côn said. She turned again to the bowl. Yên couldn't hear the words she was saying, but when Vu Côn turned around, she held out a basket of odd fruit. They were unbearably bright and colored, clashing with each other and glistening with light. They looked . . . fake, like cardboard decorations for wedding banquets.

"Here. You need some comfort." Vu Côn must have seen Yên's face. "This is what they were, before the Vanishers poisoned the world. Mangosteen. Rambutan. Carambola. Dragon fruit. Breast-milk fruit. Mango. No fungus. No rot." She sat down again, the basket in her lap. She picked out a tight, almost perfectly round shape, red as a bleeding heart and with rough, gritty skin. Her hands shifted shape, easily slicing through the thick skin and scooping out the seed. She held it out balanced on a claw. "Try it."

It tasted sweet. Too sweet, an almost-sickening explosion of juice and soft flesh in Yên's mouth. No grit, no soothing harshness. She made a face. "Elder aunt—"

Vu Côn was already holding out another fruit. "This one is sweeter."

The seeds, piled in Vu Côn's lap, were large and plump

and brown, not the shriveled ones Yên had found inside the lychees of the village orchards. She ate one, then another. The taste was settling down in her mouth: too sweet, too soft, but not wholly unpleasant. "I guess," she said, slowly, reaching out for another fruit, "I could get used to it." Her hand closed over Vu Côn's claw, held it for a moment. It took all her willpower to hold it there, unmoving, to not move upward, to touch shoulder and chest and lips.

Vu Côn smiled, and it made her appear younger and less severe.

For a moment—a bare, monumental moment of ignorance—Yên struggled with pronoun choice. She wanted to address Vu Côn not as "elder aunt" but as "elder sister." It was sheer foolishness. It was the height of familiarity, intimacy above and beyond what Vu Côn would ever allow. Yên couldn't. Instead she said, slowly, "The twins said . . . you had a duty."

Vu Côn's face didn't move. But neither did her hand. Yên felt heat rise into her heart, her face. "We're not the Vanishers," Vu Côn said. "They thought everything was playthings. That nature could be bent and rewritten to suit them. I"—her hand clenched, a fraction—"I am *better* than them."

And she'd lost everything to them, too, and to their legacy. But Yên couldn't say those words.

Vu Côn withdrew, effortlessly. "Here. You can have the last one."

Yên took the lychee, cradled it in her lap. Her hands

were smeared in sticky juice. Everything seemed to cling to her skin, including stray strands of hair from her undone topknot. She must have looked ridiculous. "Thank you," she said.

"Don't thank me." Vu Côn shrugged. And, as she moved away, Yên caught the slight swaying, saw how she held herself, trembling.

Yên was a healer's daughter, and no fool. "You're exhausted." Checking out Yên's room, the basket of fruit? Both?

A silence. Vu Côn had her back to her, but under her robes her body was lengthening again, turning serpentine, her arms shrinking, her hair subsumed into a streaming mane, scales peeking beneath her dark skin. Her hands, clenched, were now fully retracted, the thumbs indistinguishable from the other sharp, thin claws. "That will teach me to show off." Her voice was sharp and cutting, resonating with the thunder of the sea, the roars of the storm.

Yên remembered that she was talking to her jailer, to her executioner if she proved unsatisfactory. Yes, she'd been kind, she'd been considerate, but one fleeing moment of compassion didn't change what had happened. Couldn't. Shouldn't. "Forgive me. I shouldn't have said—"

"You keep doing that," Vu Côn said. She still hadn't turned.

"Doing what?"

"Apologizing."

"I don't see what's wrong about that."

Vu Côn stretched, and turned. In a heartbeat, she was the dragon again, but instead of making straight for Yên, she remained where she was. When Vu Côn spoke again, it was with the dragon's jaw. "I took you from your village. I hold your life."

All facts which Yên was all too keenly aware of. Something snapped inside her. "And you want me to yell at you? What do you expect me to do? Gainsay you in your own palace?"

The dragon's shape trembled. Yên could see the woman within it, like an insect trapped in amber. Vu Côn said, at last, "You don't have to *care.*"

"Of course I do." Yên opened her mouth, shut it again. She couldn't unsay the words. She could apologize. She—

She wasn't going to, and they both knew it.

Vu Côn shifted. She leapt into the air, heading straight for Yên, flowing over the metal floor like water. Yên tensed, knowing there was nowhere she could possibly go; but Vu Côn inflected her trajectory at the last moment, coming to rest, half-folded, by Yên's side, her maw a finger's width from Yên's mouth.

Waiting. Trembling. A moment that could be so many things. A moment—

There was no time.

Yên gave in and, bending down, kissed Vu Côn.

She tasted like the sea, salty and sharp, with a hint of earthy sand. Yên drank her in, feeling the cold spread from her lips to her face, all the way into her chest, where her heart was now a painful mass, each heartbeat magnified ten thousand times. Vu Côn's body was wrapped around Yên's chest and legs. That odd, tight wetness spreading through her clothes, through her skin until it seemed to fill her to bursting. Yên pulled away, struggling to breathe. "Vu Côn . . ."

An amused snort, filling the air between them with seawater. "You're going to apologize again."

Yên shook her head. She pulled Vu Côn close again, letting those lips engulf her, sealing all words away. She was lost, drowning beneath murky waters, lungs filled with brine and algae and oil, wanting only that coldness to fill her, to transfigure her.

And then, as the coldness wormed its way deeper and deeper into her chest, she realized what she was doing. Who she was kissing. Remembered Vu Côn walking away with Mother, casually taking her from the village. Remembered that she traded lives like coins. That she owned Yên.

"I can't do this," she said. "*We* can't do this."

And, before she could think or regret, she ran away from Vu Côn's room, and back to hers, never looking back.

5

A Slow Drowning

Yên's village was a small, dusty affair in a small, unremarkable province. Vu Côn had barely marked it when she'd been summoned the first time. Now, as she walked up its streets, she saw nothing she hadn't seen elsewhere: ramshackle buildings, small and malnourished people with the scars and sores of unhealed diseases, who were watching her warily. She didn't blame them. In the days after the world's breaking, strangers carried welcome news from outside but might also be plague carriers. She wore an isolation skin, though she had no need for it, as she was mostly immune to diseases.

Because of the isolation skin, her entrance into the village had been easy, subjected to mild decontamination protocols instead of an extended quarantine in the Plague Grove. She'd timed her arrival for market day. The guards were too busy processing traders, making sure their goods all bore the pine-and-crane certificate of decontamination from the magistrate's tribunal. A single, healthy person carrying no merchandise was barely worth a sharp word.

The twins had barely blinked when she'd said she'd be gone for a while, but of course prayers, and the occasional summoning, took her away from the palace very often. How would they do in her absence? Thông would worry about breaking the world by accident, but the truth was that the twins mostly broke themselves: arms and legs trying to climb places of the palace Vu Côn would never have thought to explore. She still remembered the time they'd found a hidden set of rafters in the gardens' towers, and Liên had fallen down, desperately trying to fly. Three broken ribs, and she was lucky it hadn't been more.

They were almost adults now. A complex, bittersweet feeling. She wasn't sure she'd done right by them—that, unchaperoned, they would fare well in the outside world.

Yên would teach them caution. She had to.

The house Vu Côn was looking for was on the edge of the village, near the oldest and most cracked section of the wall. It was on stilts, slightly higher than the floodable ground, though it was sinking into the omnipresent mud of the place. The air was sharp with despair, with unanswered prayers, with unfulfilled devotions, enough of it to make Vu Côn's skin itch. She always forgot how much she hated going out into the world: it was bad enough in the audience room, but at least there she was in control. She could put a beginning and an ending and boundaries around it. Here, she was . . . not defenseless, not as much as she'd been under Vanisher rule, but still well out of her comfort zone.

As she climbed the steps, the walls shook. She paused for a moment while the house steadied itself. Her human form was heavier than average, and the house was even more ramshackle than the usual buildings. Poor people, Yên had said, or implied. The kind who wouldn't be missed, the kind one could safely offer away.

She didn't want to think about Yên, but she was going to have to, at some point.

"I'm sorry, how may I help you?" Yên's mother stood on the threshold. With the house shaking, Vu Côn's arrival couldn't have been missed.

The isolation skin blurred her features, and in any case, Yên's mother hadn't seen her clearly. She'd already been drunk with fatigue by the time Vu Côn had arrived. "My name is Vu Côn, elder aunt. I have a message for you. May I come in?"

Yên's mother frowned, but politeness narrowly won. "Of course. I'm Kim Ngoc, younger aunt."

Inside, it was cramped and narrow. A single room gathered two sleeping pallets, a low table, and a kitchen corner.

Vu Côn handed Yên's mother—Kim Ngoc—the message, and stood for a while, one hand on the threshold. She should slip away, while the attention was elsewhere. She wasn't even sure why she was delivering the message in person, rather than just leaving it on the windowsill or, better yet, in the small shrine to the spirits in the corner of the room. That would have been appropriate. Safe. But she'd promised Yên she would carry the message, and that didn't include shying away from delivering it.

She rubbed her lips again, feeling the roughness of the isolation skin under her fingers, remembering what it had felt like to kiss Yên. Like swallowing live coals, that brief moment when a lantern's flame, plunged underwater, was extinguished; that raw, fleeting heat compressed on all sides, instantly turning to lukewarm and sending a thrill down her bones.

We can't do this.

No, they couldn't, and for so many reasons.

Vu Côn's skin itched again, a distant babble of prayers from the nearby houses. Nothing from this one: the only prayer spoken over and over—Yên's safety—was being answered.

Kim Ngoc held the paper away from her as though it might bite. Her hand shook as she laid it on the table. Her eyes were veiled with tears. Vu Côn felt her own heart being squeezed: reflex, nothing more, surely. A prayer, granted, even if she hadn't been the one it was directed at. Yên meant little to her, and Yên's mother even less. "Where did you get this?" she asked.

"It was given to me, elder aunt," Vu Côn said. "In a dragon's palace." She wasn't sure why she was so loath to lie. Respect due to old age? But she was much, much older than Kim Ngoc; older than everyone else in the village, though she wasn't about to reveal this fact through mere forms of address. "When I came to beseech for my aunt's healing."

"She says she's well," Kim Ngoc said. Her gaze wasn't on Vu Côn. "That she has students, and she's found a book no one has ever seen." A half-veiled smile. "She'd run away with my medicine books and hide in the Plague Grove. She hasn't changed, has she."

It wasn't a question directed at Vu Côn. And if it had been, she'd have to lie again.

How well was Yên, really?

She'd been burning with fever, the night she'd run into Vu Côn: she hadn't realized it, and Vu Côn had cushioned the worst of it before she'd left to examine an empty room, but she'd seen enough patients to know what she was dealing with. Pale skin and reddened eyes: not tears, either, though Yên might well think so.

She'd lied to Yên. Healthy people didn't suddenly develop magic skills, or summon gates outside of their conscious control. The sick ones, though . . .

None of the Vanishers viruses were sicknesses, in the usual sense of the term. The Vanishers had manipulated biology as easily as breathing, taking and discarding shapes and abilities like favorite clothes. Their viruses were attempts at gene-modding targets, and diseases were what happened when they went bad, as they inevitably did. Because none of the targets, whether they be human or animals, had the Vanishers' easy capacity to absorb and reshape viruses for their own ends. Spirits . . . Spirits such as Vu Côn usually walked through viruses unharmed: not because they were immune, but because the Vanishers had thought of them as servants and thus beneath their notice.

A few sicknesses caused the onset of magical powers, but most of them came with nasty side effects, if not worse. Vu Côn didn't know the name of the sickness. It might be nothing. It might be easily curable. Or—

No. She wasn't going to think on what she might have to do, if Yên's disease couldn't be cured—only passed on, to infect other people. Not going to think on what her duty would be then.

To Yên's mother, Vu Côn merely smiled, showing white, polished teeth. "She's well. Learning magic."

"Really?" Kim Ngoc looked surprised. "She's never had any talent for it. I guess everything blooms, in time."

Vu Côn clamped her lips on the "no, it doesn't" that she really wanted to say, and smiled again. Magic didn't just happen out of nowhere. There would have been warning signs—and if Kim Ngoc, who was a healer, had missed them all—then it was bad. Because the only other explanation was a virus. "I'd assume so. I can't stay long, I'm afraid. But I had to leave my aunt at the palace, so I'll have to go back. I can take a message?"

"Oh, of course." Kim Ngoc shook her head. "I'm sorry. I'm being frightfully rude. Thank you for coming."

Vu Côn shrugged. "I had business here," she said.

"At the market?" Kim Ngoc nodded. "I hope your aunt is . . . doing well?" A careful dance around the subject. She was worried. No, not quite that.

"As well as can be." Vu Côn shrugged. She probably shouldn't push her welcome. But Yên had been so desperately homesick, and she felt unaccountably guilty about the bargain she'd struck with the village. "Is there anything from here your daughter would like? Books, perhaps? Or food?"

Kim Ngoc gave her a long, hard look. "Food wouldn't keep, on such a long journey, would it?"

Vu Côn smiled again. "Depends what. Sweets, perhaps."

"She's never been much for sweets. Noodle soup, or shrimp fritters," Kim Ngoc said. "Wait here, I'll give you a message." She turned back to the lone table and hunted for paper and a brush to write down words. The paper, when she found it, was creased and grey, and the brush, thin and missing half its hairs, had seen better days. Kim Ngoc made a gesture asking for forgiveness that Vu Côn distractedly acknowledged. She'd never cared much for ceremony one way or another.

She waited, listening to the rhythm of the village, the distant rumble of the market, the itch of prayers thick in the air. Someone's self-loathing and absolute belief that justice, when it came, would sweep them away. Someone else's desperate entreaties for the harvest to be half-good, for the rice to be, if not white, free from grit and insects. A prayer for continued survival, for houses to still stand when the storms came, when the river burst its banks and rose . . .

"Here." Kim Ngoc handed Vu Côn a folded piece of paper with tight handwriting. Vu Côn barely glanced at it before slipping it into a travel pouch: she wasn't here to play prying busybody.

"Thank you." Vu Côn inclined her head, and made to leave. And then stopped, because Kim Ngoc was staring at her with dawning horror on her face.

"You."

Oh, no.

The smartest thing to do would have been to run for the open door. Vu Côn was smart, but she didn't see the point of that anymore. Instead, she threw back the hood of her isolation skin, and looked steadily at Kim Ngoc, with eyes in which the depths of the sea would be laid bare.

Kim Ngoc took a deep breath, and then steadied herself. "You're the one—"

"Who took your daughter?" Vu Côn smiled. There was no amusement in it. "You know all things have a price."

Kim Ngoc didn't move. She stared back at Vu Côn with an unreadable expression. "You didn't have to come."

"I did," Vu Côn said, gently. "I promised her."

"You—" Kim Ngoc shook herself. "She's *happy*, in that letter," she said, finally. "Here, all she thought of was escape."

Yên hadn't talked much about her life in the village, but it hadn't sounded like much of one, more like a slow, steady act of drowning, a gradual choking of the light. Not that Vu Côn had the hypocrisy to think she offered better, not when she hadn't given Yên a choice. But at least she wasn't couching it as survival of the best, or necessary sacrifices, as the elders had. "Happy," Vu Côn said, thinking of desire laid bare, and of an ill-advised kiss in the dead of the night. She kept her face expressionless.

Kim Ngoc looked up at her. There was no fear in her eyes, but it was a very different thing. Yên had stood up to Vu Côn because of outrage at unfairness. Kim Ngoc had no fear because she'd lived with so much, for so long, that she'd forgotten what it felt like to be free of it. "She wanted to be a scholar," she said. "To pass the Metropolitan exam and be escorted to the capital. To be under the Empress's protection."

Vu Côn said nothing. She could feel it, though, gathering in the air: the unspoken prayer, the desire that Kim Ngoc couldn't yet give voice to. She could have walked away. Her work, such as it was, no longer involved the granting of wishes. But instead, she found herself saying, "What do you want?"

Kim Ngoc was silent, for a while. Then she said, not looking at Vu Côn, because one didn't look at superiors, or spirits one was beseeching, "A way out," she said. "Filial piety has become chains, to her. She'll never walk away as long as she's alive."

"And will you?" Vu Côn asked, taking in the room: the healer's instruments all spread out, the piles of diagnosis and symptoms, the thick book of the Broken-World Teacher's words, shimmering like liquid silver on the bookshelves.

Kim Ngoc didn't move. "We both know the answer to that. Does a healer walk away from their patients?"

Vu Côn shook her head. "Then we both know what answer I can give you. I can't fashion miracles." She'd expected Yên's mother to crumple, or to weep or to show some kind of emotion, but the other woman's only answer was a brisk, businesslike nod. Only the tightness of her lips betrayed her.

"I see," she said. "Thank you, Teacher. I shouldn't have asked. It's for us to work out."

She looked so much like Yên, in that moment—standing, trembling, in Vu Côn's room and apologizing for the disturbance—that Vu Côn lost her composure. Before she could think on what she was doing, she'd reached out and lightly touched the woman's wrist. Her pulse was thick and complex, the flow of blood in the chest clogged around the heart, the breath shorter than it should have been. A blocked artery: an easy fix. Words flowed, from Vu Côn to her, a string of letters that shaped into an incantation, cutting through the blockage and incinerating it into nothingness. *Sword. Sharpness. Needle. Heaven's Will.*

Kim Ngoc raised her hands to her chest, slowly, carefully. Her eyes were wide open, a slow, incredulous expression slowly spreading across her face. Vu Côn hated that part. She wasn't divine, or at least not more than they were. She didn't pretend to be superior or worth worshipping. She wasn't her former masters.

She shook her head. "That's a favor. Not a bargain. And it won't last."

"What was it?" Kim Ngoc asked.

"Clogged artery." It shouldn't have been common, not with the threadbare food that was now the norm, but some Vanisher viruses had odd effects. "Your body is building it up on its own."

"The Stilling of the Crimson Mansions. It's fatal within a few years." Kim Ngoc didn't sound like someone who'd just been handed a death sentence. Merely . . . curious. "But you can remove it."

Vu Côn shrugged. "I know a few tricks."

"Sword. Sharpness. Needle. Heaven's Will." Kim Ngoc rolled the words on her tongue, as if tasting them. "They wouldn't work for me, would they? I don't feel anything, when I say them. That usually means nothing would happen if I tried to put them in a healing circle."

"I don't think they would," Vu Côn said. The Broken-World Teacher's incantations didn't depend on the language; or, more accurately, both human and spirit languages derived from the same archaic source, which fueled the spells' powers. But some spells, for whatever reason, didn't transfer from spirits to humans.

Kim Ngoc was looking at her with curiosity. Vu Côn braced herself for the roiling in the air, for the prayer she couldn't answer, the one she heard ten thousand times a day: *please make me well, please make me whole.* But there was nothing.

"You don't wish to be healed?"

"I already was." Kim Ngoc smiled. "Greediness is unbecoming. I've seen enough miracles for a lifetime." A slight itch on Vu Côn's skin, nothing more: a passing curiosity. And that same deep-seated desire, like a background to everything. Wishing her daughter to be safe, to be well. To be happy.

Happiness. Again, the memory of that kiss. Of Yên's

smile, the way it had transfigured her entire face into something strange and fragile and wonderful. Of that feeling of drinking all of Yên in, of how *good* it had felt.

No. There was no time for happiness. And it wouldn't be fair, or just, to Yên.

She needed to leave. Now, or she'd never breathe again. "Goodbye, elder aunt." She all but ran to the open door: to the village, to its miasma of ill health, of poisoned soil and broken people. To safety, never once looking back, with Kim Ngọc's message for her daughter weighing her sleeves down, as unforgiving and as cutting as sharpened metal.

* * *

Yên and Vu Côn had mostly avoided each other after . . . the incident. Yên gave the twins their lessons in the courtyard, pointing out with forceful firmness that the world had rules they couldn't afford to ignore; and all the while, she kept half an eye on the door, expecting Vu Côn to be leaning against the doorpost, watching her children with fond amusement. But she was never there.

Perhaps it was indeed for the best. Except that whenever Yên closed her eyes, she'd feel again the cold, exhilarating touch of Vu Côn's lips on hers. Except that she'd wake up at night and feel the silver letters on her hand itch, find them shining in the darkness, and see the faint outline of a waiting gate.

Magic.

Vu Côn had given her drugs, the same bitter and sharp

glass she'd already drunk. Perfumed gourd, bitter melon, and something else Yên couldn't identify. Although the fruit tasted like the lychee had: slightly off-kilter and wrong, too sharp, just enough to be recognizable but uncomfortable. She could have not taken it. After all, Vu Côn just wanted her to be a prisoner there. But the dragon had been sincere: helpful, comforting in the face of sheer malice. Desirable, and she just couldn't afford to go there.

She could have stopped, she supposed. She could have turned away from whatever strange abilities she had, and turned back to the familiar, to a world where everything was under control.

Yên was a scholar and a healer's daughter, and nothing—whether it be knowledge of history or the best way to effect a cure—had ever been gained by turning away from the truth.

And she could use it. If she could master magic, if she could do, effortlessly, more than the few spells Mother had mastered, then she could come back to the village as a magician. As a useful, valued person, one that no one would dare throw into the wilderness: a protection she could extend to Mother. When she came back, when she left the palace, when she escaped. All unattainable dreams, but it kept her awake. It kept her focused, and it gave her hope.

At night she'd read, obsessively, the book on her bedside table: ancient maxims and proverbs, the slow, painful rules of building incantations; which word combinations worked, which ones would have no effect no matter how many times she wrote them. She'd sketch calligraphy letters in the air and on the floor, and watch the letters turn from golden to ash-silver. It was draining. She had a headache that didn't seem to go away, and she woke up in the morning never feeling rested. But it was also exhilarating. Not the magic itself, but how spells were put together. How the Broken-World Teacher referenced poems and songs, how every spell called on myths and stories and sayings. How it all came together to form things that weren't just magic.

Every part of a spell has meaning, like a rite that must be followed. Words are actions and actions are words: when all is aligned, then the world will react in answer.

The spells were beautiful in their own right, like a finely written essay, singing on Yên's tongue like new year's delicacies.

Sorrow. Sweetness. Forgiveness. The taste of love.

Marriage. Promise. Red thread. A hundred knots.

One morning, someone knocked on Yên's door.

She opened it, and found Vu Côn.

The dragon was wearing a five-paneled tunic, on which her jade disk shone like the sun. She stared at Yên for a while. Her gaze was a grey, closed-off wall. She was aloof, unattainable, once more the spirit who had healed Oanh, who would have taken Mother away. Words pooled, in the darkness of her robes. *Sword. Frozen. Separation.* An almost-physical wall that Yên could feel. When she reached out, her hands pushed through thickened air.

"Here," Vu Côn said, thrusting two pieces of paper at

Yên. Her fingers rested for a bare moment on Yên's wrist, as lukewarm and as inert as stone. And, before Yên could even so much as say a word, she was gone.

"Vu Côn!"

The first paper merely said: *I gave you my word. I've kept it.* And the second one . . .

It was a smooth, grey piece of paper. The handwriting, crabbed and cramped, was Mother's, and the smell that rose from it, a mixture of sandalwood and camphor, was so familiar, Yên saw the world wobble and contract as tears came to her eyes.

Child, I thought you dead. Thank the ancestors for miracles. Here, life continues much as before. I know you worry for me, but I'm well-provided for . . . .

Vinh has learnt her letters, and is making her way through the Tale of Kiêu *with alarming speed. Khiêm is as rowdy as ever. Oanh . . . Oanh will never be the same, but she's alive. She's walking again.*

My patients are well . . . .

Little of substance there, and yet . . . Words unsaid, words unwritten. Life was going on without her. Mother was alive, and not starving or thrown out of the village.

Yên closed her eyes, trying to compose herself, and failed. She was crying, and the world was blurred and painful and raw, but it was all for the best. "Thank you," she said, aloud, and she wasn't sure if it was to Vu Côn—who couldn't possibly hear it from that deserted room—or to her ancestors, or to whatever spirits remained in the Heavens.

She tried to find Vu Côn, to thank her properly. But when they did meet—in passing, at one of the twins' lessons—the dragon was aloof, unattainable, exactly as she'd been on the doorstep. They'd broken something, when they'd kissed. And the only things Yên felt was sorrow that it hadn't lasted longer, and anger that Vu Côn was letting it all die out. Pathetic.

And yet . . .

* * *

Vu Côn stood, uncertainly, at the door. The curtain whistled in the breeze, grey and tattered and eaten through by moths. She stared at it. Time to turn back, to begin the slow trudge back to the palace, back to her patients. Back to Diêm Châu, who was progressing so well: when Vu Côn had told her the next time she'd be ready for the full healing, the little girl's smile had been wide, like a rising sun, an odd, twisting feeling in Vu Côn's chest. Most of the people she saw couldn't be cured, or not durably. Most of the healings that succeeded left people scarred and changed, hollow ghosts of themselves. A drop of water in the ocean of trying to undo what the Vanishers had done. And yet she had to try. As Hoang had said: if they didn't, if they just let the world die from roiling poisons and sicknesses, then what made them any better than the Vanishers?

Diseases. Poisons. Gene-modding viruses.

Vu Côn thought of Yên, standing outside her room. Their hands, touching. Warm, pliant skin, sending a shiver up her spine. And that brief moment of lingering on Yên's wrist, which burnt her desire to bitter ashes in a fraction of a breath. Yên had been pale and thin, but that could have been worry. The pulse, though—small, and pathetic, so thready and weak Vu Côn could have crushed it with her bare hands—the pulse didn't lie. And neither did her spell. On Yên's wrists, the letters shone so strongly, they'd lost all color and depth, fighting endlessly against what was burning within Yên. Against what was destroying her.

Any illusion she'd had that Yên's disease was going to burn itself out had died then.

Noises came from inside the house. Bangings of pots and porcelain, and another voice cursing. Not the right time. Vu Côn turned away to leave, the village's prayers a distant irritation on her skin.

"Elder aunt?"

Kim Ngoc stood on the threshold, uncertainly. "I wasn't expecting—"

Vu Côn shook her head. She wasn't sure why she was back, what kind of thread had drawn her, as surely as a fated bond, back to Yên's village.

"I don't want to bother you," Vu Côn said.

Kim Ngoc snorted. "Never."

Inside, two people were busy. One of them was an elderly person, wearing the faded robes of a scholar and with greying hair tied in a topknot. The cut of their clothes marked no gender. They were watching a pot of stock on the stove. The other was wearing a traditional woman's ensemble: a white tunic split at the sides of the waist, and black silk trousers. She was busy taking down shirts from a clothesline. Oanh, the girl whose healing had given Yên to Vu Côn. She looked better than she had on that night, though she still moved as though carved from glass, as if her skin were merely the thinnest of cloaks on muscle and bones. Vu Côn's words of healing still clung to her wrists, almost faded now, absorbed by the body.

Neither of them showed any sign of recognizing her. Good. She didn't need any more trouble, not when everything in her was screaming at her to get out. From the scholar came a prayer, a stronger, sharper one that she'd heard before: a desire for justice and a complex acknowledgement and acceptance that they would be judged for their part in things too, something too elaborate for Vu Côn to grant, a perpetual itch at the back of her mind.

Kim Ngoc introduced Vu Côn as a traveling merchant, and the elder as Giang. There was the usual chatter about the land, the capital, the court of the Empress, the distant hierarchy of temporal power Vu Côn cared little about but which Giang clearly hungered for. Oanh contributed little.

Finally, Elder Giang withdrew their pot from the stove, and laid it on the table. "Supper is ready," they said. They pointed to another, covered pot. "That's the rice. And the vegetables are in that one. Come on, child," they said to Oanh.

Oanh looked as though she might protest.

"Grandmother Ngoc has a patient," Elder Giang said, with a sharp look at Vu Côn.

Vu Côn opened her mouth to say she wasn't sick, and then closed it.

After they'd left, Kim Ngoc spread two bowls and chopsticks on the table, and opened the pots. The smell that wafted up was familiar, and yet so completely off-kilter, tinged with the earthy notes of mold.

Vu Côn ate in silence. When she was done, she carefully balanced her chopsticks on the rim of the bowl, and said, "Yên said it was just the two of you."

"Before Oanh's healing? It was." Kim Ngoc sounded amused. "Guilt is a powerful motivator, isn't it."

"How are you?" Vu Côn asked. She gestured, with her hand, toward Kim Ngoc's wrist. Kim Ngoc nodded.

Her pulse was strong, with just a tiny hint of the clogging building up again. Vu Côn shook her head. "You're better than I expected."

Kim Ngoc shrugged. "I'm not a spirit, but I do know a few tricks."

The small, ineffective remedies the village folks had passed on to each other. "I see," Vu Côn said. She kept her face neutral, because to speak up would be needlessly hurtful. "Well, ask me again in a few months' time. It's too early to clear it again. It would damage the artery for very little gain."

Kim Ngoc sighed. She poured tea for both of them, a black one, redolent with a different smell of mold. Deliberate this time, the leaves carefully tended to cultivate the flavor. Such things had existed before the breaking, though Vu Côn preferred her tea grassy and green, with subtle flavor. It probably wouldn't have survived the water if said water was drawn from the river.

"I'm well," she said. "It's odd, to not feel out of breath anymore. Or to wake up, and there's no pain in my chest."

"You were lucky," Vu Côn said.

"That you happened by?" Kim Ngoc smiled. "Is that really luck?"

Vu Côn didn't know, not anymore. How much of it was fate, and how much their own actions and choices, and if there were any difference. "You should leave," she said.

"There's nowhere to go." Kim Ngoc gestured toward her leg, the one that kept slightly dragging on the floor. "Do you truly think I'd run fast enough to avoid the constructs?"

"No one does," Vu Côn said. "A traveling merchant could take you to a bigger city. . . ."

Kim Ngoc sighed again. "You're a healer, aren't you? Would you leave your patients?"

"Of course not," Vu Côn said. It was gut reflex, as unthinkable as the sun rising in the west.

"Exactly." Kim Ngoc sipped at her tea. "It's not so bad. The children come too. Yên's students. They bring little things. Leaves. Paper. Books. And as long as I'm useful . . ."

More useful than her daughter, the life they'd offered up, as thoughtlessly as they'd discard dust. The life Vu Côn was still holding. In more ways than one, because she hadn't yet told Yên how bad it was. Because she didn't know how bad it was, and wouldn't know until she'd examined Yên more thoroughly.

"You're just playing into their hands."

Kim Ngoc raised an eyebrow. "No. I refuse to play by their rules. I refuse to decide who is valued, who is not. To trade favors. Isn't this what healers should do?"

Of course. Vu Côn didn't favor one person over another. She didn't treat anyone differently. Though some of the children, feverish and still struggling to smile, would break her heart into so many ugly, jagged pieces.

Vu Côn said, slowly, carefully, "They'll kill you."

"Yes," Kim Ngoc said. "One day. But that's the way things go, isn't it? In a world where we're all weighed on how much value we bring, and seen as burdens when we're no longer of use."

Usefulness.

You're smart and handsome, and I hate waste.

A life, held because the twins needed it. Not because they'd die, but because of what they'd do, if left unchecked. Teaching them passion and the love of decorum, because she needed it. For the sake of the world—of her children—dismissing what it cost Yên of little importance in the grand scheme of things.

Usefulness. Burdens.

"Not everyone is like that," Vu Côn said, with a sinking, leaden feeling in her throat.

"It's the worst part of ourselves." Kim Ngoc set her cup on the table. Only a scattering of droplets lay at the bottom, like a string of darkened, shriveled pearls. "It's always with us. Always whispering. Always calling. And sometimes, we answer.

"Why are you here, elder aunt?"

Vu Côn opened her mouth to say she didn't know, and found no true words in the emptiness of her mind. Because she knew why she'd come. Because of Yên, in a way. Because the last time she'd been there, Kim Ngoc had assuaged her guilt. Had told her that Yên was better off in the palace than in the village. Had given tacit approval to her indenture of Yên. She'd come back for that. For ways to rationalize what she was doing, all of it from the lies to Yên's servitude.

She rose, draining the last of her cup. "I'm here because I shouldn't be thinking like that."

6

Sleepers

Yên was late, and angry, and lost.

She'd gone to the small, twisting garden where she usually taught the twins. The day's lesson plans had not been thrilling: reading *The Pearl and the Scholar* together, an elaborate moral tale about a scholar falling in love with a fisherman—and the fisherman's quest into a Vanisher's holdings when, years later, the scholar contracted a virus that split his soul—so that the âm part of him wandered the world, gathering knowledge, while the duong self endlessly, forlornly wandered the Vanisher's palace, looking for his missing love.

It wasn't subtle and it wasn't fascinating, but the verses were beautiful, and the myriad word choices and allusions were a great opportunity to explain, at length, what friendship and duty and love meant. And, in the end, after many travails, the lovers reunited—and, in the long summer evenings when the fisherman was out working, the scholar's âm self would sleep in their bed, while the duong self would wander once more, watching his love bring up nets of shrimp and fish from the river's oily waters.

Yên expected Liên to protest at the unfairness of the lovers' years of separation, trying to find a solution, and Thông to thoughtfully consider the matter, dissecting what both the scholar and the fisherman had done wrong and how they'd brought this hardship on themselves.

Except that the twins hadn't been in the garden at all.

She'd gotten the day wrong again. Not an uncommon occurrence in a palace where not much deviated from routine. But she'd tried the other teaching places. The courtyard, the corridor with the infinitely receding windows of skyscapes, even the library, where she found the door tightly locked, and no noise or light within. The twins were nowhere to be found.

Off again on their adventures, maybe? But they'd never missed a lesson. Vu Côn had made the consequences of that clear. And even clearer to Yên what the consequences of non-attendance would be.

Vu Côn would have her head. The panic was old and reflexive now, almost written over by the memory of cold seizing her lips, running like a shiver up her spine and stretching her entire being with unattainable, unreasonable desire.

She needed to keep her wits and find them. Fast.

Unbidden, words rose to her lips: a spell she'd seen in the book, one to find lost relatives. And didn't the First Teacher say that teachers and students might as well be parent and child?

Her hands moved before she could think, tracing the letters in the air.

Blood. Bone. Threads. Fated to meet again.

The letters on her hands burned, silver turning to a crisp white. The sharp, merciless radiance of the unbroken moon: the one under which the Vanishers had once hunted, whipping their servants ever onward, driving their prey to blood-streaked exhaustion and death. The floor under her, a single window into an impossible world, shifted, the words she'd spoken replacing the blasted and pockmarked surface. They twisted, then became the spirits' language, and then fragmented, abstract signs, as if the palace itself was digesting what she'd spoken into a more palatable state.

Blood. Bone. Threads. Fated to meet again.

Something tugged at Yên's guts, like a fishhook digging into her innards. It traveled upward into her heart, pulling slowly but steadily. She was already walking. Running, because it kept mindlessly rising, dancing on the edge of pain.

Blood. Bone. Threads. Fated to meet again.

A large corridor, the wind rising and whistling through angled stairways that led nowhere. A garden that folded back onto itself: the path she traveled on got her back to the doorway she'd entered by, except that it now led to a different room. A scholar's studio that kept climbing upward, the latticework windows twisting and turning until they were the floor on which she walked; and through them she could see another scholar's studio with the same eight trigram windows, the same inkstone, brush and scroll pots, and cut-bamboo wrist rest . . . .

The pain in her chest was flaring up again. Not constant or fixed, but moving like a burning brush, sweeping across the space of her entire body. And then it flared so strongly, it almost sent Yên to her knees—and, just as abruptly, snuffed itself out like a spent lantern.

Yên looked up, and there was a door, a handspan away from her face.

It didn't look like any of the doors she'd seen before in the palace. The other doors had been small and narrow. This one was huge, a layer of filigreed grey metal over a flat panel that must have been bronze or copper, a rich brown color that peeked through the filigree, shading into golden and red on the edges of the doors. Birds and trees and dragons, twined around abstract patterns. No, not abstract. They were words, written in the spirits' alphabet, and not growing infinitely larger or smaller, but merely written in a tight, cramped hand, barely visible under the layers of ornamentation.

When Yên laid a hand against the paneling, the door lit up in a harsh green. A sound started, on the edge of hearing, one that turned her innards to jelly, making her shiver where she stood. Turn back, she had to turn back before it was too late. And then that too passed, leaving her struggling to stand.

The light died. The doors swung open toward her, ponderously and noiselessly. There was time to turn back, to the relative safety of known areas in the palace. But then she heard the thread of sound. Two voices, unmistakable. The twins, arguing. They were too far away for her to make out precise words.

Inside, darkness stretched, thin, faint filaments of light hung like spiders' webs. Yên couldn't see the walls or the room. A kindness, after everything else in the palace. But then her feet caught on a raised protuberance on the floor. For a moment she felt herself fall, desperately trying to catch herself, and then she was on the floor with a skinned knee and a burning sensation spreading to her entire leg. Amazing, wasn't she. A clumsy peasant oaf. The twins would never waste a moment reminding her of this . . . .

Light flooded the room. Yên looked up. She had to blink, lest she be blinded. Everything seemed to be unbearably sharp, outlined in ringing lines that contracted, hurting her eyes.

Close to her, close enough to touch, was a bed about her size: a contraption of polished metal and glass that held one sleeper, their skin faintly glowing from within, motes of light shifting on their arms and legs, faint traceries of letters in that same alphabet. And, to either side of it, the translucent shape of larger beds and larger sleepers. All the beds were identical, all the sleepers different though arrayed in the same pose, flaring out in size and receding, as if the bed Yên was looking at was only the part of a circle closest to her. And, in the distance, at what would have been the halfway point of the circle, the beds shifted, shrinking in size again, growing farther and farther away from her.

It should have sent Yên to her knees, struggling not to vomit, but it was all so huge and so faint that it didn't seem real. The only thing at her scale was the bed in front of her, which held one sleeper. Human, or human-shaped.

Where were the twins? She could hear their voices, but they didn't seem to be anywhere . . . .

Then something caught her eye, to the left of the bed. In one of the infinitely receding series of beds, she saw two small shapes, arguing.

How—? She tried staring at them again. Nausea was rising, this time her brain trying to tell her that it was all real . . . .

Yên gave up on subtlety. "Children!"

In the small scene to her left, the twins looked up, startled. She saw them make a gesture with their hands, caught something that might have been "Teacher," or her full name.

The entire ring *heaved*. There was no other word for it. All the beds seemed to move like boats caught in a storm, bobbing up and down and sideways, receding and growing as they slid sideways—stretching and altering, so that the sleepers grew taller, their faces slightly melting, like sealing wax. Yên looked away, the nausea in her throat sharply climbing, trying to steady herself by staring at the steel floor.

She was still looking downward when something slid into place with an audible click. "Teacher! What are you doing here?"

Yên looked up. Liên and Thông were standing by the side of a bed, but the occupant of this one wasn't sleeping. They were sitting up, their skin blackened by burns, on a pale skin the color of yellow apricot flowers. They smiled at her, in that uncertain way of people who weren't certain what the proper behavior was.

"This is Gia Canh," Thông said. "Yên is a . . . guest of Mother's. Our teacher."

"I see." Gia Canh's voice was rich and resonant. His eyes—he had used the masculine to refer to himself in Viêt—were black, with pearled blood at the edges of his eyelids. It had gone beyond faintly creepy, and into something else altogether. "A guest, too?"

Yên turned. Forced herself to, because the view was still dizzying and wrong. "You live here?" she said. She saw, suddenly, on one of the beds, a familiar sight. Even in the distance, the faces were unmistakable: the father and his child, the ones who had walked away into nothingness during Vu Côn's audience, so long before. "No," she said. "You asked her for a boon. The dragon."

"You didn't?" Gia Canh's voice was mildly curious.

Of course she hadn't. Of course. "What did you ask for?"

"What we all ask for." Gia Canh's voice was bitter. "To be healed and made whole."

She stared at him, hard. Saw the slight trembling of his hands, the way the blood at the edges of his eyes had seeped into the whites of his eyes. His duong self was overlarge. When he moved, Yên could see, not the

119

faint shadow she'd seen with the child, but a limning of fire around the planes of his face, an energy that pooled within him with no outlet to escape.

"It's called the Sorrow of Monkey and Rooster," Thông said, quietly. "A bloodborne disease that snuffs out the metal in a person's khi-elements. There is no cure."

The sleepers. The beds. "This is a hospital," Yên said, flatly.

"A death-house," Liên said. She sounded angry. "Most of those who beseech Mother . . ." She stopped, then started again. "Mother repurposed the Vanishers' berths. They used them for genetic manipulation, but we can use them to induce stasis. To hold time and sickness at bay. That's why we live here."

"Cryogenics," Gia Canh said. The word meant nothing to Yên. He sighed, again. "It's like the worst sleep you've ever had. Like something sitting on your chest, gobbling up your lungs piece by piece. Slowly choking to death in the midst of nightmares. But you're alive." He didn't sound in the least bit happy about it.

Liên was bent over the side of the bed. Yên realized that some kind of control panel was open, with commands displayed in glistening light. The alphabet was utterly unfamiliar. Vanisher words? "I think I've got it," Liên said, to Canh. "This is going to drain the excess duong from your body. Ready?"

Gia Canh looked at Yên, and then back at Liên. His face was taut with fear. "I don't think I can take much more of this," he said.

"One more time," Liên said. "Please. It should work."

Gia Canh sighed. "What I wouldn't give to be cured." His voice was low, the amusement bitter and sharp. "One more time. But afterwards, you have to ask your mother."

"You have my word," Thông said.

"Ask what?" Yên asked, before she could think.

"To wake," Gia Canh said. "To take what little time I have walking through gardens, listening to rivers and watching the fullness of the moon. To breathe in the flowers and the laughter of children. I can't sleep anymore. Not like this."

Letting himself die. Yên had seen it, numerous times, in Mother's patients. Mother had argued, had tried to convince them to fight, but in the end, she had to admit what any healer did: that the patient's wishes prevailed. Vu Côn was likely in that same denial.

A hospital. A healer. Yên hadn't thought—no, she'd known, she guessed, because Vu Côn had healed Oanh, because she was treating Yên. She'd just never followed the thoughts to their logical conclusion.

Gia Canh lay down on the bed again. Liên touched the symbols, one by one. Something shimmered in the air above him. His face twisted in terrible pain. A scream formed on his lips. Yên moved to touch Liên, but Thông was already there, slamming their hand on the symbols.

Nothing happened.

Gia Canh's scream tore through the air, a high-pitched, unbearable wail. Blood was spreading across his face. No, not blood, but something dark and sticky, a shimmering vermillion that turned his eyes the color of an imperial seal. Yên tried to reach him, but her hand hit an invisible barrier, again and again.

Liên's face was white. "It shouldn't be doing this!"

Thông spoke words in a language Yên couldn't understand. It hung in the air: signs that grew larger and larger, syllables that pressed against Yên's ears and eyes and nostrils until all she could see and breathe was the echo of that word. Something wet was in her face: she wiped away drops of blood.

She couldn't hear Gia Canh's screaming, but his hands were moving, clawing at the glass, the same vermillion tinging his fingernails. His fingers warped. She couldn't hear the snap because of the words Thông was speaking, but she saw them move into impossible, limp angles, even as his face twisted and twisted again.

Liên screamed. It was the same language as Thông. Yên's left eardrum ruptured, fluid leaking into the hollow of her ear. The symbols on the panel shifted, for a fraction of a second, and then went dark. The barrier above the berth snuffed itself out. Gia Canh slumped back like a broken puppet, limbs askew. As the echo of the words died, and Yên's world gave way to a piercing, unbearable pain, she heard his fast, labored breathing. But she was on her knees, trying not to scream herself.

Hands steadied her. Liên, kneeling by her side. "It'll pass," she said. "Breathe."

Yên tried to, but it hurt too much. "What happened?"

"It didn't work," Liên said. "The berths are for gene-modding, same as the viruses. I thought we could rewire them with the right base pattern, and…" Her voice trailed off. "Mother is going to kill us."

Yên breathed again. The world refused to steady itself. "Rewire," she said. It was the only word in her mind.

"We've been doing that since we were kids," Liên said. In the distance, Thông was speaking in a low, urgent voice to Gia Canh.

In, out. In, out again. Memories bubbled up, from another lifetime, from Mother's manual and the far-away village. She'd have given anything to be back there. Things were bad, then, if she was nostalgic for the elders' enmity. "My eardrum. It's ruptured, but it'll heal itself, won't it? Unless it becomes infected."

"May I?"

Yên nodded. Liên's hand brushed her hair. More words, this time ones that Yên could barely recognize. *Farsight. Ant. White-throated rooster. Rot beneath walls.*

A tingling of warmth. "It should be fine." Liên breathed out. "How is he?"

Thông had stopped speaking to Gia Canh. "Come and see," they said. And, to Yên: "Don't touch him."

Gia Canh's body was now so pale, it was almost translucent: not pale skin, but a uniform, waxy color with no distinctive features that was profoundly unnatural. His eyes were closed, his breathing labored. The vermillion hue was almost gone. Only on his eyelids and on his fingernails was it visible at all, a network of thin lines like blood vessels, or cracks in a celadon dish. It shone, faintly. A single, luminous word hung on his chest, the one that both meant strength and fullness of health. His duong self was dull; his face had the darkness and translucency of dominant âm.

"How is he still breathing? The berth?"

Thông shook their head. "The spell." They laid a hand on the glass lid of the berth, tracing the contour of the word. Faint lines went from it to the duong organs: the large and small intestine, bladder, stomach and gall-bladder, and a larger, fatter bundle of lines to the middle burner organ. "It's regenerating his duong, but it's very slow. He needs to pull through the night." They didn't sound happy. Or optimistic.

Liên's face was taut. "It's our fault. We never should—"

Thông's voice was gentle. "He knew the risks, and he agreed."

"You mean we're not guilty?"

"Of course not. We totally are. I mean we take our responsibilities, but we don't let it eat at us. We can't afford to, lil' sis."

Liên took a deep, shaking breath. "All right."

Yên said, in the awkward silence, "When you say 'don't touch him' . . ."

"I don't think he's contagious," Thông said. "But I'm not keen on having one extra patient."

Yên started to say she didn't know the twins were healers too, and then she remembered what Liên had said, about Mother having their hide. "Gia Canh agreed to being healed by you, but you're not *allowed* to do this, are you?"

They looked, not at Gia Canh, but at each other. At length Liên said, "Please don't tell Mother."

She was supposed to. She couldn't afford not to. "Just so you can avoid punishment? I'm your teacher. I'm not exactly supposed to help you bend the rules."

A silence, again. Thông said, "We'll tell her. Tomorrow. We just need a chance to make things right."

And then Liên, whose hand was trailing, lightly, on Gia Canh's burnt face: "Tomorrow, we'll know whether he has a chance. I want to know what we're apologizing for."

Yên thought for a while. They were her students. Her responsibility. But, looking at their crestfallen faces that barely masked shock and grief, they were punishing themselves enough. And the prospect of going to see Vu Côn—of *talking* to her, as if the kiss had never happened—twisted her stomach in knots.

"Fine," she said. "Tomorrow."

* * *

When Yên came back to her room, she found Vu Côn waiting for her.

So much for avoidance. The dragon wore not her five-paneled dress but a large tunic split over silken trousers. The tunic itself was the dark brown of the earth, long enough to trail on the floor, pooling around Vu Côn like fallen maple tree leaves. Words glittered in its folds, changing too fast and too abruptly for Yên to follow. The air was thick and cloggy, as if before a storm.

The word "master" rose and died on Yên's lips. Instead, she bowed, falling to her knees on the floor, head touching the floor: the full obeisance, as she'd once done before Vu Côn's throne. "Was there anything?" she asked.

Silence. A rustle of silk. And hands, wrapping around hers. Looking up, she found Vu Côn, kneeling by her side, her robes spread around her in a glory of star-studded darkness. Her eyes were the depths of the sea, the depths of the sky, the hungry maw that always sought sustenance, and Yên was as nothing before that. She was drawn, inexorably, stripped bare of everything. Of duty, of filial piety, of knowledge, of words.

"Lil' sis," Vu Côn whispered, the single word echoing under the vast ceiling. It tightened in Yên's chest like an unbearable noose, a weight suddenly shifting and reconfiguring the entire universe. *Lil' sis.* A familiar pronoun used only between intimates. "You're no longer my servant."

"I don't understand," Yên said, and the words died as Vu Côn's hands tightened around hers.

"I'm sorry. It should never have happened in the first place. You're free." Vu Côn rose and drew Yên up, effortlessly, as the words on the floor, in the cloth, shone like wildfire. On Yên's wrist, an answering light, that of the spell Vu Côn had laid on her.

Yên looked for words. There were none. "The twins. You need someone to teach them—"

"They'll survive." Vu Côn's face was grave. "You can stay here and study books of magic. Or teach the twins, if that's what you want. Or go home, though I'm not sure it's best for you."

A chasm yawned beneath Yên. For a moment, the future was so many things, so many flowers she could pick. It should have been exhilarating, but it wasn't. It was just bone-deep fear, a loss of certainty, of the walls that had not only bounded her but defined her existence. *I don't know*, she wanted to say, but the words remained stuck in her throat.

Vu Côn let go of her hands and withdrew, the coils of her tail sliding across the polished floor. "You can't be leaving," Yên said. So many things she wanted to say. To yell at Vu Côn, to tell her she couldn't just treat Yên as a plaything, and in the end the only one that came through was how much Yên just *wanted* the dragon.

Vu Côn didn't move, though Yên now saw that the dragon held herself still only through a great effort of will. "We need to talk," she said. "And sleeping with me out of gratitude isn't—"

Yên covered the distance that separated them in a single, agonizing heartbeat, one that felt as though it were tearing apart her ribcage, resonating until her entire body ached with need. "Don't," she said. "Do you want this?"

"Yes," Vu Côn said. "But—"

Before anything could change, Yên grabbed Vu Côn and kissed her.

She tasted like the sea, like the storm: tangy and bitter, the coldness on her lips like a jolt that spread from Yên's mouth to her lungs. Yên's breathing was slow and painful, and then lost altogether as she breathed Vu Côn in. Her hands, fumbling, found the fastening of the tunic and slipped it from Vu Côn's shoulders, revealing golden-dark skin, just as Vu Côn's own hands undid the clasps on Yên's shirt. Vu Côn took off the slender sleeveless undershirt, slipping it over Yên's head in one fluid movement. Wind whistled on Yên's bare, exposed skin: wet cold creeping up her skin like fingers, gently stroking the hollow between her legs, her hips, her chest, circling her breasts until she shivered and gasped.

Vu Côn's face lengthened and changed, the antlers sprouting from her head, her mouth now filled with glistening fangs, but the bulk of her scaled body remained human in shape. Her snout brushed Yên's lips, again and again; it nipped at the nape, at the top of the neck until Yên's entire being seemed to be inarticulate moans. The cold was rising to drown her: the sea and the storm encasing her, not numbing her limbs or fingers, but making everything sharp and sensitive, on the quivering edge of painful desire. She stroked Vu Côn's antlers: a soft, silky touch, Vu Côn shuddering every time Yên's fingers trailed upward.

She was on the bed with no memory of getting there, looking up as Vu Côn unfolded. The huge coils of Vu Côn's tail held her legs, slimy and wet and oh ancestors she'd never hungered for anything so much as that touch, pinning her in place. Above her was the dragon, mane glistening against the infinitely receding ceiling; droplets of water were floating down to Yên's bare chest like finger-strokes, a slow, agonizingly slow trail of icy fire from her navel to her breasts while within her desire crested, vast and terrible and utterly unbearable.

Vu Côn's words shimmered, in the darkness. *Hunger. Desire. Folly.*

I don't care. Let me have this, please. Just this thing. One night. One moment of breathing that belongs just to me. And, reaching up, Yên drew Vu Côn to her, and drank in all of her to slake her thirst.

7

Threads of Fate

Yên woke up to an unfamiliar presence. For a bare, panicked moment, she thought she'd opened a gate again, that whatever lurked behind the threshold was in her room. And then she remembered, and the cool, soothing languor stole over her limbs again.

She lay in the crook of Vu Côn's arms, pillowed on wet scales. Cold had seeped into her hair, a tingling, pleasant sensation.

"You're awake," Vu Côn said. She lay with her head on Yên's lacquer pillow, the points of her antlers barely resting on the sheets, the rest of her body spread, serpentine coils taking over the entire bed. Her gaze was still far away. "Last night..."

Yên took a deep trembling breath, found herself braced for unpleasantness. "It was wonderful," she said, trying to still the shaking of her body.

Vu Côn's clawed fingers trailed in Yên's hair, gently untangling knots. "I hadn't done this in a long time." Her voice died away, no longer old or severe, but full of a terrifying, childlike wonder.

Since Vu Côn's husband had died. Yên closed her eyes. The water from Vu Côn's body seemed to have crept into them, a stinging pain she couldn't blink away. "It was worth it," Yên said. So many questions, so many unsaid things. She was free now, free to leave the palace, to return to her village. To Mother and her duties. To the elders. She could take the book with her, continue to work with it until she mastered the magic. Until she could avoid accidentally opening gates—

No, she wouldn't think of the gates, or of what waited for her on the threshold.

"We do need to talk." Vu Côn sounded regretful. She bent toward Yên, kissed her lightly on the lips, sea salt and cold, tight air, and a faint aftertaste like algae.

Yên said nothing, merely waited. It had been wonderful, and yet it changed nothing. Not to who they were, not to what they'd done. She might be free, but she was still a poor scholar, and Vu Côn was still a spirit in a palace, so immensely beyond Yên, the *idea* there might be more than one night was presumptuous. Vu Côn was so brusque and so accustomed to getting her way, so unthinkingly arrogant that she'd never consider Yên as more than a passing fancy, a toy she could have. They could have that night, and more besides, but it would never be more than an affair. Yên had her own duties, her own life.

And then there was the matter of whatever the twins were up to, of Gia Canh and the hospital and the sleepers' room.

When Vu Côn did speak, it was nothing Yên expected.

"Your mother is a healer. You used to assist her. You must have basic knowledge of the five elements and the flow of khi in the body."

"Yes," Yên said, cautiously. Was this about the hospital? Was she meant to help there? A covert way to let her know Vu Côn already knew about the twins' experiments? But Vu Côn's face was drawn, taut with something almost like grief.

"Have you taken your pulse lately?"

The implications were obvious. Yên said, "I leave that to people who know what they're actually doing."

"Humor me," Vu Côn said. It would have been an order if her tone hadn't been so bleak. And then Yên remembered she was free.

Yên sat up. Moving away from Vu Côn felt like tearing herself away from the numbing, reassuring cold into suffocating dryness. She laid a hand on her pulse. Under her fingers wasn't the regular throbbing of a human heart, of blood shifting from liver to heart, from veins to arteries. It was faint and crumbling like dry rice cakes put in the mouth, disintegrating into stale dust as soon as the tongue touched them. Her duong and âm were still in balance, but they felt curiously loose, not tied to each other as they should have been, as if a slight gust of wind, a slightly stronger-than-usual breath, were going to be enough to send them both tumbling into nothingness.

On her wrist, Vu Côn's words shone. Blazed, more strongly than ever. Protecting her, Vu Côn had said. Making sure she had time to master the magic. But that wasn't all they were doing, was it? A fist of ice was tightening around her innards. She withdrew her hand from her wrist, took her pulse again. That same fluttering, irregular feeling. Every moment felt like a struggle, every moment wondering if it would finally flounder and stop.

"I'm ill," she said, slowly, carefully. Which was . . . no, not impossible, because everyone fell ill, because of course she was, else why the medicine Vu Côn was giving her, or the words on her skin? "It's serious."

Vu Côn had pulled herself up. She was naked still, her long hair streaming behind her, halfway to a mane of hair and greenish algae, her skin soft and pliant. Yên ached to lose herself in it, knew that she couldn't, not anymore. "I'd need to examine you to know. In my office."

Unbidden, a memory: Vu Côn, standing on the threshold and handing her Mother's message. Remembered a hand as inert as stone brushing her skin. "You've taken my pulse already, haven't you? How long have you known?"

Vu Côn shook her head. "I wasn't sure when you developed the magic. Those things just don't happen to adults. It meant you'd caught a virus somewhere. The magic is in your genes now. It's unlikely healing you would remove it. But the virus is still raging in your body."

"And you never told me?" She shouldn't be yelling. She shouldn't be so angry, except that here it was: Vu Côn deciding on what was best for her, thoughtlessly, not even realizing what was wrong with that. Like the words on her wrists, except that these had been to keep her out of immediate danger, and this was just denying her the truth. Just watching her dance near the abyss.

"I had it under control."

"That's not the point!" Yên struggled to breathe. "I want to *know*, not to be protected like I'm a five-year-old child!"

Vu Côn drew herself up, eyes blazing. Her antlers grew two sizes larger, sharp enough to transfix Yên, and matters would have been very different if someone hadn't knocked at the door, the sound echoing in the deathly silence.

They knocked, again and again, getting increasingly frantic. "Teacher? Teacher? Are you here? Please."

Yên and Vu Côn stared at each other for a fraction of a second. They both dived toward their discarded clothes. Yên slipped on her tunic and trousers as the knocking went on. "I'm coming!" Behind her, Vu Côn was rising, clothed in scales and whirlwind and the murkiness of algae. When Yên threw open the door, Vu Côn was one step behind her.

It was Thông, disheveled and out of breath: their flowing, embroidered tunic hanging askew, with the sleeves of their under-robe peeking out from the brocaded ones. Their gaze moved from Yên to Vu Côn, taking in their own disarray. A brief, eyebrow-arching moment before they remembered what had brought them there. "Please," they said. "He has Liên. He—he says we owe him, that he wants to get out of the palace—" They breathed, slowed down, but all the words came out in a jumble. "He's all pain and anger, and I don't know how to stop him!"

"Who?" Vu Côn asked, but Yên already knew the answer.

* * *

"Tell me again." Vu Côn's voice was icy cold.

Yên clung on for dear life. She and Thông were riding on the back of Vu Côn's huge serpentine form, zooming through a corridor, pillars rushing by in a thunder of vermillion wind. Vu Côn's spines rubbed against Yên's fingers every time she banked.

In Yên's mind, her spell for finding the twins ran, again and again. *Blood. Bone. Threads. Fated to meet again. The youngest.* She'd amended it to find only Liên; otherwise, she'd have been overwhelmed by the proximity of Thông, who was sitting next to her on the dragon's back. The answering tug was so weak, she couldn't even pinpoint a direction.

"I've already—" Thông's voice was small and slight.

"—told me that you decided to try healing someone on your own, and then when that didn't go right, decided that I didn't need to know and you could fix it yourself?" Vu Côn's growl threatened to unseat Yên.

Yên said, "I was going to tell you." She fought back the urge to cough. She felt increasingly lightheaded and exhausted from the exertion of clinging to Vu Côn's back.

Vu Côn growled again. "You're not the one who has

to apologize." She banked again as the corridor made a sharp turn.

Thông said nothing. They weren't in full dragon form, presumably because Vu Côn wasn't about to allow it. Though now that Yên thought about it, the twins were reluctant to shift shape at all. They'd playfully take on dragon attributes, but she'd never seen them as she'd seen Vu Côn: huge and serpentine, all sharp edges and spines and claws.

Around them, the walls receded, and the room with the sleepers shimmered into existence. The huge, ornate doors, and ahead, the ring with the infinitely receding beds; the single empty one with its controls glowing in the darkness. It shimmered, as if it weren't quite there.

"The bed isn't here," Thông said, quietly. They sat on Vu Côn's back, ramrod straight, though their discomfort seemed more embarrassment and fear. "We're halfway there."

"There's no one here," Yên thought. Liên. Flighty, fearful Liên. "When did he take her?"

"I don't know," Thông said. The same hint of panic in their voice she'd heard back at the door, alien and frightening. Thông seldom panicked. "He struck me unconscious as he left. He must have thought Liên would be more tractable. . . ."

"Breathe." Vu Côn's voice was calm and controlled, like a skin stretched taut over a drum moments before it broke. "When did you come into the stasis room?"

The ghostly bed rushed at them. On either side were

sleepers—human, or human-shaped, with creases under their eyes and skin blackened by burns, hands resting by their sides, fingers slack, nails tinged with the faintest blue, eyelids pale and closed. They were odd and unnerving. Yên suddenly realized it wasn't because of their shape. It was because they didn't move. Because their chests didn't rise and fall, because they showed no sign of reacting to the dragon's presence, because they didn't look like they were sleeping.

Thông said, finally, "It was the end of the bi-hour of the Cat."

"Half an hour," Yên said, aloud. Vu Côn's spines were digging wounds into the palms of her hands. "They can't have gone far." She forced herself to breathe. Her mind seemed to have scattered. Still no answer from the spell, and breathing *hurt*. This time, the cough came unbidden. She swallowed but nothing seemed to ease the constriction in her throat.

Sick. She had no pulse, or close enough.

Vu Côn rumbled again, under her. "I've warned you not to over-exert. You're—

"—ill," Yên snapped. "Yes, I know." And there were so many things about that they needed to discuss, but now was not the time.

"Mother," Thông said. "I could—"

"Yes," Vu Côn said. She didn't sound happy. After a silence that went on for far too long: "That's not up to me. But I trust you to make the right choices."

"Do you?" Thông asked, and Vu Côn had no answer.

Yên remained silent. It sounded far too large for her to wade into without knowledge.

"She can't open the gate," Thông said. They took a deep, shaking breath. "Only you can." That last clearly to Vu Côn. "He'll kill her."

Yên felt the shudder that went through Vu Côn's body. "There has to be a way. . . ."

"There is," Thông said. Their gaze was distant, their laugher bitter. "We've already breached so many rules of decorum. We might as well go on as we have started."

It made no sense to Yên.

Thông drew themself up. As they did so, their entire shape seemed to shift and lengthen and change, scales flowing up from their hands to their face, the bare outline of antlers shimmering into existence, their hair streaming in the wind, covering Yên and Vu Côn in glistening darkness. "Show me," they said, and their voice was like thunder, making the entire palace shake, and Vu Côn buckled, as if in pain, below Yên. Yên's hands tightened, and still she started to slide down, her stiff fingers betraying her. Thông spoke again, and the vermillion pillars around them bent inward. Vu Côn screamed, and it was clearly pain this time, twisting in Yên's entrails until it seemed to be her own.

"Take me to where my sister is," Thông said.

A rumble. The pillars shook and cracked, with a sound that rolled away from them in both directions. The entire corridor sagged, as if all the bearing structure had come down. Cracks spread through the pearlescent walls, through which a bright, blinding light shone: that same yellow one Yên had seen in Vu Côn's room, except ten thousand times harsher, the fire that would end the world.

Steps appeared in the corridor, but on all four sides, growing larger and larger as they led away from the walls, the space between them leaving less and less margin for Vu Côn to squeeze through. They were going to be crushed.

"Child," Yên said, to the towering shape of Thông. A coughing fit stopped her.

Thông looked at her, and smiled. It was . . . almost familiar, gentle and amused, and yet something with it was so completely, jarringly wrong. "It'll be fine," they whispered.

Ahead, the stairs had joined, forming a vertiginous braided corkscrew, an impossible geometry that refused to coalesce into anything meaningful.

"Show me," Thông said, again in that voice that seemed far larger than it had any right to be. This time, the tremor in Vu Côn's body was barely perceptible. Yên couldn't feel anything: Vu Côn's protective spell, perhaps? All she could think of was Liên, was that time was running out.

Thông laughed, a sound that shook the corridor again. Slowly, ponderously, the stairs moved, opening up like a flower, revealing the liquid silver shape of a mirror in their center. A door. It rippled, as if to an inaudible rhythm. No, not inaudible. Yên heard it now, rising through the invisible pillars: a song as hesitant and pure as a child's tune, and as hauntingly familiar.

She didn't have time to ask herself what it was, because Vu Côn, without a word, raced toward the opening. Silver rushed to meet them all, the door growing larger and larger, each ripple the size of a tsunami, and everything flashed black.

A moment—a stretched, painful heartbeat when she couldn't breathe, couldn't move—when she saw a dim shadow in the distance, growing larger: the silhouette she'd seen bending by her bed, the sheer, unending malice, and Vu Côn's words burning on her wrist, trying to keep it at bay . . . .

No.

Please, no.

And then time snapped back into place like a pulled rubber band, and the world rushed back to fill the void. She was on her knees in the dirt, coughing and coughing and coughing, struggling to breathe. And then it passed, leaving her almost too weak to stand.

She had to.

Because the other thing she could feel was the tug in her gut, rising now, unbearably familiar. Liên. She was close enough to Liên.

She pulled herself up, shaking. Neither Thông nor Vu Côn were anywhere she could see. And . . . She glanced around, but the malicious presence she'd felt in between the gate and wherever she'd landed wasn't there, either.

She was in a sphere, like the library: a huge, translucent room with curved walls, rising slowly towards a dizzyingly faraway closure. Except that instead of pillars, the spheres held trees. They were sharp, skeletal networks of wires planted on the inner surface of the spheres, climbing upward as the walls did, dotted at regular intervals, a strange and distorted grid that almost made sense—bad imitations of life, shapes thinned and cut until they lost all substance and all semblance of pleasantness. Vanisher trees.

It didn't matter. Yên set off at a shaky clip, going in the direction of the tug. It rose as it had, previously, a sharper and sharper pain in her heart, a growing constriction in her lungs. Hard to tell, anymore, what was the sickness, what was the spell.

Blood. Bone. Threads. Fated to meet again. The youngest one.

She was going deeper and deeper into the forest, into the gardens. Trees rose all around her, swimming into sight, a devastation of cutting edges and unnaturally thin branches. Here and there, a few slender tree shoots looking similarly elongated and thin, sharp edges with nothing of life to them, no lichen, no fungus, no moss.

Blood. Bone. Threads. Fated to meet again. The youngest one.

Liên.

Breathing hurt, and her legs wobbled, and she was going to be sick, but she was the only one who seemed to be anywhere close, and there was no time. Around her, the trees tinkled. The noise should have come from the glass spheres that hung levitating a finger's breadth from the branches—fruit, or liquid, or both—but it seemed to well up from the heart of the skeletal trunks.

The ground curved up. Yên was on the inside of the spheres now, clinging to what should have been the walls—*don't look down don't look down.* The voices had fallen silent, and the air was now oppressively hot. Not good. Yên pushed herself harder. The ground between the trees was now strewn with saplings. She wove her way through them, acutely aware the smallest of them would transfix her feet through the soles of her shoes with the same ease as a spear. Her lungs burnt, her legs wobbled. She wasn't going to hold on for much longer.

And then she rounded a clump of trees into a clearing scattered with saplings, and saw two shapes. The pain of the spell flared up, and died. Yên remained upright, but it took all she had.

There.

One of the two shapes was Liên. She lay on the ground, unconscious, with a bruise spreading across half her face, the scales scattered across her left cheek turning dull and lusterless. The other had to be Gia Canh. But when he straightened up and turned, dragging Liên with him like a limp doll, wrapping his hands around the curve of her face, Yên barely recognised him.

His limbs hung crooked and out of shape. His skin had been marred by burns before. Now it seemed to be an ocean of suppurating sores, sheening a sickly yellow in the light below the spheres. His duong self pulsed, weakly, within him: he was almost all âm now, and in terrible pain.

"You," he said, to Yên. "Younger aunt. I hadn't expected

to meet you again." His voice was no longer pleasant and low, but raucous. Damaged vocal cords. But no, that wasn't just damage. That was someone peeled raw, whittled away until only pain and fear remained.

Liên hung in Gia Canh's grasp like a broken thing, arms and legs at impossible angles, skin darkening to the color of bruises. Gia Canh's hands were wrapped around the curve of her jaw. Just one move downward, and he'd snap her neck. At his feet, shadows pooled, words drawn from the trees, moving and shifting, opening and closing like flowers in a frenzy to blossom and die. "Let go of her," Yên said.

"You don't understand."

"I do," Yên said, slowly, carefully. "You're badly hurt. You're angry. There's no need to drag her into this."

"Drag her? *They* dragged me into this. They made this. They—" Gia Canh's voice was shaking. "They broke me."

"You agreed to it!" Yên said, and then realized it was exactly the wrong thing to say. "Look," she said, extending her arms. She wanted Thông to be here, or Vu Côn. Someone who'd know what they were doing. "I'm sorry about what happened to you, but do you think this is going to make anything better?"

"*Nothing* is going to make me feel better." Gia Canh's voice was feverish. "You don't understand, do you. They'll put me back in the beds. They'll stuff me back in with the sleepers. An eternity of being in stasis, and nothing to take away the pain. I can't. I just—" He shook Liên as if she were a thing. She moved with him, limp and completely,

143

jarringly relaxed. Yên fought the urge to run and snatch her from Gia Canh's grasp. She wasn't going to be fast enough. "You don't understand. I want to go out. I want to see the outside. Trees and rivers and places that make sense, not this—this monstrosity of palace!"

Yên spread her hands again. "I can't open a gate. She can't either. You know this."

Liên still wasn't moving, but color was flowing back to her face. Yên saw her eyes open, for a fraction of a heartbeat only, before they closed again. But it was because she held them shut, not because she was unconscious again. Playing dead, and likely as drained as Yên felt.

"I don't care. Get me out of the palace," Gia Canh said, and he sounded almost as though he were pleading now. Lips clenched, anger and fear and longing all tied together. "Away from the beds. Get me out, or I'll kill her."

Yên didn't have much. Magic, now almost spent. She was exhausted, body and mind, and none of the spells she'd read in the book would come into her thoughts, everything blurred and unattainable. No. She had nothing that could help.

And yet. And yet, if she did nothing, Liên was going to die. She'd seen patients like Gia Canh often enough, and she knew that pain had taken him far enough that he'd do anything to make it cease. Do something, and do it now.

But she had nothing, and no one . . . .

No.

That wasn't true.

She had Liên.

"Liên," she said, slowly, softly, knowing that Liên could hear every word. She spread her hands, bracing herself to run. He could snap her neck so easily, but deep down, he had to know that it was irrevocable. Once it was done, he had no bargaining power left.

"Stop," Gia Canh said. "Move back." His hands tightened. Liên convulsed, starting to choke.

"Change!" Yên screamed at Liên, and ran.

Everything seemed to happen at once. Gia Canh's hands tightened further, pressing down so strongly, they went white. A scream, and Yên realized, halfway there, that it was hers, had always been hers. A snap of broken bones—no, there wasn't. A clink of scales, and instead of Liên, Gia Canh was now holding a smooth, serpentine shape. Yên covered the rest of the distance while Gia Canh's brief shock wore off. Liên was writhing in her other shape, trying to wriggle out of the hands that still kept her enclosed. Yên reached both of them, and flush with her momentum, bore them both to the ground. A confused scuffle, Yên's hands finally closing around Gia Canh's hands, tearing them away from Liên's neck. Liên, slithering away, leaving Yên trying to fend off hands and feet that seemed to be everywhere.

"Teacher!" Liên's voice. Yên batted away a hand that tried to gouge out her eye, and tried to find a purchase. Something. Anything. Gia Canh kept slipping away from her. Whenever Yên managed to find a purchase, Gia Canh would slip or tear out of it.

And then the ground shook, beneath her. "Let go of her," Thông's voice said, far away.

Something grabbed Yên and pushed her upward, away from Gia Canh. His hands slid away, grabbed her wrists, and wouldn't let go.

"I said, 'Let go'." The anger in Thông's voice was unmistakable, but it felt wrong, too, as if something were pushing nails into Yên's ears. "Leave us alone."

Yên and Gia Canh held each other. He was on his knees, struggling to push himself up. The words from the trees pooled under his feet, shifting and changing, growing darker and darker, and the pressure on Yên's wrists stronger and stronger—until something snapped, and Gia Canh let go of her, tumbling toward the ground, breathing heavily. Under him, the earth was dark. No. It wasn't darkness, but his blood, his fluids. It was clinging to him, drinking him dry: all that remained of his duong first, and then the âm, turning his skin from the grey color of the rotten moon to a featureless translucency, like the wings of a butterfly's corpse. His face turned upward, but he wasn't staring at Yên, but at something beyond her. "You," he whispered, and the pronoun he used was archaic, one Yên had read in books but never heard. "The masters . . ." His voice dipped and sank, and became inaudible as he pitched facedown on the ground, and didn't rise again, his body shriveled and dried, like the husk of a man.

The masters.

No no no no.

Yên rose, shaking, to face Thông.

They didn't look like a dragon at all. Why had Yên ever believed they were one? Their hair streamed around them like the mane of a lion, with the polished shine of lacquer. Their face, elongated and stretched, closed on a fanged snout, but the eyes were too high and too close, stretched into oval shapes rather than almonds. The scales were the color of rusted buildings, except that they could be seen faintly behind the translucence of the sclera. The body was serpentine, but it had too many arms and legs, all sharp claws and disjointed fingers; and all of it kept shimmering, as though not quite in focus, changing shapes, sprouting more scales, more legs and more arms. And the antlers . . . the antlers were the branches of the trees around her, sharp and frightening, as if someone had distilled the essence of knives and razors into thin lines.

"You're—" She wanted to say they were another spirit, something in Mother's storybook, a ky lân or one of the myriad spirits that must still be walking the earth. The words remained stuck in her throat. Because she knew in her bones, in her lungs, in her guts—knew, just as her ancestors had once known—she knew what she was facing.

Vanisher. They were a Vanisher.

Liên. Liên was behind them, except she wasn't the woman Yên had taught, but a sharp monstrosity: a smaller, more compact shape with scales shining oily and wrong in the gardens' light, antlers like knives' blades, rusted with dried and blackened blood, shimmering and changing and alternating between dizzying shapes, each of them as twisted and *wrong* as the previous one.

She stood next to Vu Côn. The dragon was in human shape, watching Thông with that same dawning horror in her eyes. No, that wasn't it. There was wariness in her eyes, but no surprise.

"You killed him," Vu Côn said.

"The palace did." Thông's voice was still too resonant and deep, that same sense of wrongness that shook Yên to the core, and now she knew why.

"Child . . ." Vu Côn was weeping now.

Thông seemed to shiver and shrink, and the towering shape that held Yên pinned in place became that of a person again: the same genderless face with the flowing robes of a scholar, and the long, disheveled hair. "Lil' sis . . ."

Liên had shrunk too, back to her human shape, though the shadow of antlers remained behind her head, flickering in and out of existence with a faint hiss, as if they were puncturing the dome's air over and over. "I'm all right," Liên said. She didn't sound like she was.

Vanisher.

They were both Vanishers.

And Vu Côn stared at Thông with only worried affection, and held Liên against her like a mother would hold a child, with no hint of rejection. "You knew," Yên said, shaking.

Vu Côn stared at her, and said nothing.

She'd known they were Vanishers. She'd known Yên was sick. She—she hadn't said anything. She—

"Come," Vu Côn said. "Please, lil' sis."

It should have made her happy, that form of address. From lover to lover, from friend to friend, from equal to equal.

She couldn't breathe. She couldn't think. Everything was folding and tightening around her, and darkness was stealing in, as inexorably as Gia Canh's am and duong had been drained out of him. How could she trust Vu Côn to examine her? How could she trust her with anything?

"No," Yên said. "Stay away from me. Stop hiding things. Stop making the decisions for me. Just stop." And, before she could think, she started to run. Stumbling at first, and then gaining speed, weaving her way between saplings and trees, not daring to look back. It was stupid and pathetic. They might be exhausted, but all they had to do was shift to their other shapes, to flow, liquid and elegant and graceful, between those sharp, unnatural trees. Or just to run. Every breath in her lungs felt like fire, and any moment now she was going to cough again, and have to stop lest she choke . . .

She couldn't possibly hope to escape.

On her wrist, the words Vu Côn had drawn blazed, sharp enough to burn. Constricting her. Imprisoning her. Making decisions for her.

Ahead, the trees tinkled: those impossible fruit floating below sharp, unforgiving branches, and the surface of the spheres, overhead. A wave of homesickness rose in her like knives, tearing her apart. She wanted to be home. To be in the small streets of the village, where she knew the shapes of all the houses, the bends of the river, the gates of the gardens and mansions. To her and Mother's small, crooked house, away from the village's life. To the smell of garlic and jasmine rice, not the odd, strong smells in the kitchens, everything familiar honed and concentrated into sickening.

Behind her, the wind rising, and Vu Côn's voice, getting closer, "There's nowhere you can run. Lil' sis." Broken and pleading.

The pain on her wrist was getting unbearable now. Shaking it hadn't changed anything, and she was now biting her lip not to cry out. Blood flooded her mouth. Yên lifted her hand with the word, rubbed it against her lip, again and again. Pain crested, ebbed away again. She drew a deep, trembling breath. Her throat hurt, and the air didn't ease the pain in any way. She coughed, again and again—slowing down to an agonizing crawl, as the world folded itself again and again around her, everything blurring—the trees and the spheres and the grass that shone like bladed metal—raised her hand, again, to her mouth, as if she could rub away the constriction in her throat and lungs.

Ancestors, please. I just want to go home. Please.

"Lil' sis." *Do not look back, do not look back.*

Please.

Blood smeared the words on her wrist. She felt it like a red-hot brand on her skin, a jolt that sent a scream tumbling out of her lungs. She pulled it away from her lips, staring dazedly at the throbbing surface. The words, blurred almost beyond recognition, winked, as words in the book had once winked at her.

Scholar. Return. Threads. Fated to meet again.

Her hands moved, tracing them in a daze. Something tore, within her, like the tug she'd once felt when looking for the twins, except a hundred, a thousand times as strong, as if her guts were suddenly pulled through her piece by piece.

And the world tore in answer.

Scholar. Return. Threads. Fated to meet again.

Ahead, a dark slit appeared between two of the trees, widened to become a door. And, waiting on the threshold, the dark presence she'd felt twice before, a twisted mass of claws and teeth waiting to claim her. To tear her apart and rend her.

It looked like Liên, like Thông, like a smaller and pathetic version of what she'd seen in the gardens. There was no intelligence or sentience in its gaze: merely hate and malice and hunger. Its hair was short and almost shorn, its face so thin there was only one eye, and a mouth full of entirely too many fangs. The body stretched like a snake's, like a dragon's, dozens of legs sprouting out of it.

A construct. A gatekeeper. A chimera the Vanishers had made to guard their doors, to frighten humans and spirits long after they'd left the earth. A being of sheer spite that lived to kill and maim and shed blood.

It didn't frighten her, not anymore. Everything she feared was at her back now. Bleeding, her breath burning,

Yên ran toward the door she'd just opened, weaving her agonizingly slow way toward the waiting shape.

It grabbed her as she passed, hissing like a maddened snake, its claws raking the side of her body. Nothing would go through.

Yên punched it, again and again. Blood streamed down her hands, her fingers. Pain was an abstraction now, a thing that existed in some other world beyond the haze. "You're. Not. Stopping. Me." Again, and again, as it held fast. Its claws dug into her arms, sought her chest, her face, her neck. She punched it again, and it fell, crying out.

Scholar. Return. Threads. Fated to meet again.

Yên tore herself away from its flailing limbs, and walked, slowly and shakily, deeper into the gate. She should have run. She couldn't hope for more than a few stolen moments. She should have run . . . .

She stumbled, and then there was nothing but an endless fall into darkness.

8

Âm and duong

Vu Côn found Yên's body in the gardens. Behind her, the gate she'd opened was slowly drawing closed again. The keeper on the threshold was gone, faded as soon as Thông and Liên had approached: not keen on facing its makers or what remained of them.

Vanishers.

If she closed her eyes, she'd still hear Thông's voice, commanding the palace to obey them. She could still feel the words ringing within her, reminding her of times when these words had held her in place, when they'd lashed out like whips, drawing blood like red mist on the floor. She'd still see Liên, drawing herself up, the oily scales on her skin fading away, shivering and weeping and incoherent with fear.

Not now. She couldn't afford to break, not now.

There were things to be done, first.

Yên was pale, her skin almost translucent. She was cold to the touch, almost all duong and no âm, weighing next to nothing as Vu Côn lifted her. She hung, limp, in

Vu Côn's embrace. Vu Côn had briefly taken her pulse, and felt only the faintest trace of a rhythm: an odd, syncopated one she couldn't quite place, but that was most definitely not a normal heartbeat.

"Here," Thông said.

Vu Côn said nothing and walked on, her feet ringing on the polished metal of the floor.

"We can help," Liên said.

Vu Côn shook her head. She didn't speak again until Yên was lying on a steel table in her laboratory, wrapped in one of the blankets Liên had embroidered, back when she'd still been trying her hand at cloth. The lopsided birds glared at her as she sat down.

"She should be in stasis," Thông said. They'd used the laboratory's foundry bowl to brew some tea. They handed a cup to Vu Côn, and another one to Liên, before they settled down with their own, crouching on their haunches on the floor, watching her.

"She's not going anywhere," Vu Côn said. She needed to do what she'd said she would. To examine Yên, properly, figure out what was wrong with her, how to fix her, if she could fix her at all. If she could fix the deeper wrongs: the merciless moment when Yên had turned away from her with a betrayed look on her face and run toward the open gate, fighting the gatekeeper she'd so feared rather than come back to Vu Côn.

You knew.

Stay away from me. Stop making the decisions for me.

"You should be in your room," Vu Côn said. Everyone

was dancing around the subject: the unspoken words, the unvoiced fears.

Liên's laughter was bitter. "Locked doors? Do you think they'll hold us anymore?"

Thông was staring at their tea.

Fine. If no one was talking about it . . . Vu Côn was feeling raw and exposed, but she'd never shirked from her duty. "You killed a patient," she said to Thông.

"Who was about to kill Liên. And Teacher Yên." Thông's voice was distant, toneless. Shock, or did they simply not care? Did the act of taking a life mean as little to them as it had meant to their genitors?

How much had she failed, as a parent, as a protector of the world?

Liên said, finally, "The Sorrow of Monkey and Rooster. He was contagious, Mother. You kill the infected."

"Yes." Vu Côn forced herself to remain icy cold, because if she paused for even as much as a moment, she'd feel again the pain her masters had once inflicted on her. "Do you think this was the same?"

Liên opened her mouth, closed it again.

Thông drained their cup in a single gulp. "Of course not. This is the palace. You kill the infected in the outside world, to prevent further contagion, or those who can no longer bear the pain and ask to die. Here, there's no one they can contaminate. We put the sick in stasis." Their voice had the singsong accent of a lesson learned by heart.

"He didn't want to go into stasis," Liên said.

Gia Canh had tried to kill Liên. Truth was, in the

same situation as Thông, she'd have killed him herself in a heartbeat. But it would still have been a mistake.

Vu Côn knelt by Thông's side, stared at them. They'd always be the small, slight child she'd found in the breeding grounds, their eyes too big for their face, dark tears running down their cheeks as they said "Mamma mamma" over and over again. They'd always be the toddler clinging to her legs as she tried to examine patients: the preternaturally serious child announcing they wanted to be a doctor and memorizing all the symptoms of all the illnesses in Vu Côn's medicine book. *Her* child. "Listen to me," she said, lifting Thông's head to stare at her. "He wasn't about to kill Yên. He was barely clinging to her. You could have moved them away from each other with a flick of your fingers. But that's not what you did."

A silence. Then Thông said, not looking at her, "I didn't mean to. I didn't think. I just wanted him to go away." They took a deep, shaking breath. "But the palace doesn't care, does it? It . . . just thought I wanted him gone. For good."

Vu Côn didn't answer, because there was no need to.

And, after a pause, Thông said, "How do I make sure it doesn't happen again?" It broke her heart, because she had no answer to that question.

"It won't happen again," she said, but her certainty was lies. They were what they were, and a single one of their words shook the palace to its foundations. She'd known this. She'd raised them, knowing what they could do. And, desperate to find Liên before it was too late, she'd let

Thông speak to the palace. She'd opened the floodgates, and now Gia Canh was dead, Yên was unconscious, and how was she to make everything better again?

* * *

Yên lay on something cold and damp, struggling to breathe. She tried to get up, but she had no strength. Demons wove in and out of her field of vision: beings with teeth and claws, and then they shifted, and became the many-limbed, sharp monstrosity of Liên's Vanisher shape, slipping out of Gia Canh's grip and joining Vu Côn—

No no no.

"Child?" It was Mother's voice. She. She had to be hallucinating. She couldn't be back home. She tried to speak, but her lungs felt gummed shut. "Help me!" Mother said, at someone she couldn't see.

A brief, intense argument. Then Mother's voice, calmly stating what was going to happen. Yên couldn't hold on to any words. Every time she tried to focus on something, the world contracted and fuzzed again. In the background, blurred and distant, Thông and Liên were looking at her, once more human and looking drained and frail.

A flash of darkness. Then she was lying in a bed in a familiar room. It smelled of camphor and lemongrass, with a faint aftertaste of rice. The walls were bamboo, and above her were the distant rafters of the thatched roof. The wind sang through the holes, a comforting, familiar tune.

Home.

She was home.

She ought to have wept, or rejoiced, but she couldn't even muster the energy for that. Shadows hovered at the edge of her field of vision, becoming the deep, sweeping trail of Vu Côn's clothes, on the edge of shifting into a tail again, becoming Vu Côn's eyes, burning into hers . . . .

She fell again, into darkness.

In her dreams, she lay upon the cold, merciless floor of the spheres. A heartbeat, and then the dream shifted, and Vu Côn was carrying her, as effortlessly as she'd carry a child. *No*, she said, *no*, but no muscle would answer her, and all she could do was lie, limp in the dragon's embrace—staring at the twins walking by Vu Côn's side, holding each other's hand as if afraid they would vanish—at Thông's somber face, at Liên's torn and burnt clothes and the way she held herself, fragile and hurt, like a child huddled after a fight.

No. Vanishers. They're Vanishers.

She had to remember that. She had to remember that Vu Côn had known. That she'd never told Yên anything. That she couldn't be trusted, that she would always ignore Yên's desires and fears, always do what was best for Yên or others without actually *asking* . . . . She had to hold on to something, to anything, but the world kept sliding away, again and again.

When she woke up again, drained and hollow, Mother was sitting by her side.

She'd changed, but Yên couldn't pinpoint how. She'd expected—she'd feared—that Mother would become frailer and more ethereal, but the grey hair, pinned into a topknot, looked much the same, as did the aquiline face, in which she could trace her own features.

"Where—"

"We found you on the steps." Mother shook her head.

We? Before Yên could speak up, floorboards creaked, and Elder Giang came into view. "Child." They didn't look happy. "I see you didn't follow my advice." Behind them was Oanh. Yên's friend was almost unrecognizable, sharpened into skeletal thinness, her skin darkened, with a scarlet tinge like blood.

Yên's wounds had been bandaged, but she still felt lightheaded, and her lungs still afire. A heartbeat was all it would take for the fever or the cough to return. She tried to speak, found her throat was burning.

"She shouldn't be here," Elder Giang said. "You know the other elders—"

Mother's voice was steel. "Did you want me to dump her in the wilderness and leave her to die there?"

"You know what I mean," Giang said. "They barely tolerate you as it is. If they find out you broke the village's quarantine laws, that you're sheltering someone they sold away into servitude . . ."

If they found out, it wouldn't be just the wilderness. It'd be the purifying circle, for her, for Mother. "Leave me," Yên whispered. Every word felt like raking her throat dry, and a cough wracked her entire body. For a moment she felt herself dying, struggling for breath and finding none. And then it passed, leaving her wrung out and exhausted.

"Oh, child," Mother said. She was barely holding back tears. "You need to care a little more about yourself and your own happiness."

How, when just a moment of getting what she wanted—a single night of sated desire—had so catastrophically backfired?

"Save your strength," Mother said. Behind her, ghostly shapes. Vu Côn, lining up instruments in a faraway room, lifting a needle to an invisible light and watching it sheen a cold, merciless blue. Thông, pacing the floor, reciting diagnoses and surgery procedures, and Liên, her hair tied behind her, looking something up in a book. "You're not well. And there's certainly no question. I'm not abandoning her again."

She had to say it. "Contagious," Yên said. It took all the strength. She fell back, exhausted.

"I don't think so," Mother said. She frowned, as if trying to decide how much she should tell Yên. It didn't really matter, because the shadows were growing again: Vu Côn's face lengthening, becoming that of a dragon again, the twins Vanishers, and the gate shimmering in the background, waiting to lead her back to the palace, to Vu Côn and everything that had happened there.

No. She was out. She'd escaped. She'd rest and recover, and do what she should have done in the first place: run away into the wilderness rather than endanger everyone else. She didn't have the book anymore. She felt its loss like a loss of her own self, but she had the magic. She could do some spells, and even the gates didn't scare her anymore. She'd find a place that would take her.

The world contracted and fuzzed again, and the darkness closed in from all sides. She didn't so much lose consciousness as let go, sinking into a place where pain and worries didn't mean anything anymore.

* * *

In her dreams she was on a hard metal surface, while above her, red and blue lights blinked. She tried to get up, struggling to breathe through lungs that seemed to have shriveled away, but Vu Côn was there, pushing her down, holding her gently, rocking her back and forth. Everything was fractured and slightly distorted; and cold, so cold, as if all warmth had been leeched from her bones, leaving her brittle and exhausted, utterly drained of thought or gestures. In the distance, a slow, rhythmic, obsessive sound, stuttering, again and again, until she found herself listening, waiting for it to fall forever silent.

"Shhhh," Vu Côn said. "It'll be all right, lil' sis. I have you."

And then she was lying in another bed, in another room. In Mother's patient room behind a hastily drawn curtain, listening to faraway voices. Except that the sound she'd heard wouldn't fade away: a halting rhythm, always on the verge of failing. And she knew, suddenly, what it was.

Her own heartbeat, magnified ten thousand times until it made the walls of their small house tremble. She lay back, listening to it. She'd have asked how bad it was, but she didn't need to. Because no one healthy had that kind of rhythm in their chest. It wasn't just the weakness, but it was completely irregular.

What was happening?

Outside the house, the life of the village was going on. Yên could hear people calling to each other, the laughter of children in the streets. Were some of these her own students? And, in the distance, the sound of rice pounded in pestles.

In the other room, only silence. The liquid sound of tea poured into three cups, and the sharp, moldy smell wafting up to her. Then, Oanh's voice: "I don't know what happened, but—"

"She's scared." Mother sounded . . . angry, as if she'd made a mistake somewhere. *Don't be*, Yên wanted to tell her. *It was my own fault. Because I trusted Vu Côn. Because I'd wanted it so badly to be true. Because I'd needed to feel happiness so badly after so long without it.* But speaking was too much of an effort.

"She escaped," Oanh said.

"We don't know that," Elder Giang said.

Mother said, slowly, "She said she was setting Yên free."

"When?" Giang's voice was sharp. And, when Mother wouldn't answer: "Then all we have to worry about is the elders."

"And the disease," Oanh said. "Have you forgotten she's sick?"

"*I* haven't," Mother said, mildly.

"How—" Elder Giang paused, and started again. "How bad is it?"

A silence, filled only by Yên's stuttering heartbeat. The floor itself trembled, a shiver that seemed to be all of Yên's world, and a growing cold in her limbs. Vu Côn's embrace had been cold, but this was different. This merely told her she'd never feel warm again.

"She's got what I had," Oanh said, softly. "Doesn't she? The symptoms . . ."

"They don't all match, though it could simply be a mutation," Mother said. "She's almost all âm. Her duong is completely exhausted, and it's choking her. And her heartbeat is odd." She paused, then said, a little hesitantly, "It's fast and slippery, but there's this sort of echo to it. Like the pieces of a mirror."

An echo.

Yên lay back, and listened. Her own heartbeat. Her own life, slipping away as she lay on that bed. *Focus focus, hear only the rhythm. Like a healer, seeing the body first, the person second.*

Mother was right. It was two rhythms. The first faltering one, and a second one on top of it, even weaker than the first one. A fraction of a second after the first one, like a call-and-answer. As if she had not one but two pulses.

She tried to lift a hand, to check her own chest, but she had no energy for it. Two pulses. That was new. She hadn't heard it, before passing the gate. Her own disease, progressing? Or had Vu Côn heard it already, and simply chosen not to tell her?

"You think she's growing a second heart?" Oanh asked.

"I don't know," Mother said. "It doesn't seem to come

from a second organ. It's just superimposed. If there's a second one, it's quite close to where the heart normally is. I can't be sure without opening the chest. And . . ." A pause. "That reminds me of something, but I can't remember what. I've seen this before, or heard of it, in a different context. . . ."

Her chest. Her life. Yên was just too tired to care, too tired to hold on to it.

Giang sucked in a breath. "What Oanh had didn't have a cure. Except—"

Mother's voice was hard. "If it comes to that choice, I'll summon the dragon again. And give her a piece of my mind while I'm at it."

No no no. She couldn't. Just the thought of Vu Côn walking into the house. Of her gaze, surveying Yên's meager possessions, meager existence, weighing Yên, deciding what she was worth, whether she was worth saving . . .

Please, no.

Outside, the noises of the village had fallen silent. All Yên heard was footsteps on dry earth. A child's voice, excitedly saying something about a body in the mud. And the voice, calmly answering them, telling them that the problem would be dealt with.

Elder Tho.

Body. Arrival. Mud. Her. That was her they were talking about.

They were coming for her. And this time, they would finish what they had started: not leaving it up to a dragon and her quixotic ideas of servitude, but executing Yên and Mother and the others.

She. She needed to get up. She pushed with all her strength, but her limbs didn't answer her. The footsteps were mingling with her own faltering heartbeat now, strong enough to make the house vibrate.

Get up.

The room was growing dark again, and her chest was burning, except she couldn't even cough anymore. Just choke, in the growing silence.

Get up.

In the shadows, shapes coalesced and then came apart again. Serpentine and fluid, they might have been Vanishers or dragons. They might have been Thông or Liên, or even Vu Côn.

Get up.

Don't, Yên thought. *Magic.* There had to be something she could do, with her dim memories of the book. But she had no energy left for that. Instead, she put everything she had into the act of getting up. And, measure by measure, she did: pulling herself trembling and shaking to her knees, just as the footsteps crashed down on the stairs at the house's door, and Elder Tho's voice said, "Now, what do we have here?"

* * *

Vu Côn went to see Diêm Châu, before she operated on Yên.

The little girl slept under the glass surface of the sleeping berth, unaware of anything that went on outside of it. Her face was set in a grimace. The stasis was neither pleasant nor restful. But it preserved. It healed. It extended lifespans.

Vu Côn ran a hand slowly, carefully, on the berth. "I'm sorry," she said. She didn't even know if Diêm Châu could hear her. "There's something I need to do before I can take care of you. But I haven't forgotten you. I'll heal you. I promise."

There was no answer. She hadn't expected one.

She walked back slowly to her laboratory, and sat for a while, staring at the darkness.

Yên was still lying where Vu Côn had left her. She'd woken up once, screaming and thrashing, and Vu Côn had rocked her back to sleep, pressing her down on the table until Yên fell silent again. Now she was sleeping again, unaware that Vu Côn was there, or deriving any comfort from her presence.

Though would Yên have been comforted, or repulsed? The look on her face, as she'd run away from Vu Côn, from the palace . . .

No. Vu Côn couldn't afford to think of this, or she'd never do what needed to be done. She had to focus on duty.

On the smooth steel surface of the foundry bowl was the diagnosis she'd entered a few hours ago, after examining Yên. The White Tiger, Changing, its letters flowing in the spirits' alphabet. Ironically, the same thing that had brought her to Yên's village: an illness that destroyed the khi-metal in the body, causing deep, fatal exhaustion.

She only had to send it through: to command the foundry bowl and be presented with the array of things she would need to operate on Yên. Acupuncture needles, scalpels and knives, thread to sew it all back together when she was done.

It might well kill Yên. But, if she did nothing, Yên would die anyway. She thought she could live with the risk, but in truth, just the sight of Yên lying cold and breathless—just the thought she and Yên would never speak again—tied knots of ice in her guts and squeezed until everything hurt.

Behind her, footsteps: Liên and Thông. Liên looked better, wearing an elegant tunic in red silk with embroidered flowers and peach tree branches, her skin with a scattering of scales, her face slightly longer than usual, with the shadow of a snout.

Thông looked despondent. Their deep purple robes were folded and rumpled, something they'd never have tolerated in better circumstances. *Oh, child.*

"Do you want tea?" Vu Côn asked, because she didn't think they'd bear a hug at that time.

Thông nodded. "How is she?" they asked.

"The same." Vu Côn reached into the foundry bowl, sending the commands for tea. Three celadon cups shimmered into existence, full of a deep grassy-green liquid. The smell of leaves filled the room, banishing that of disinfectant for a bare moment. "How are you?"

"The same." Thông didn't even smile.

Vu Côn watched them drink the tea in silence. She

said, finally, "You asked me what you'd do, to make sure it doesn't happen again."

Thông's head came up, sharply.

She'd had time to think about it. A sleepless night that felt like a wake. A moment, stretching into eternity, holding Yên down as she'd hold down any other patient, except that it was Yên and that she'd think of kisses and naked bodies if she allowed her thoughts to stray. "You're doing all you can," Vu Côn said. "And maybe it's your fault, maybe it's the palace's fault. I don't want to attribute blame. It's pointless. It's not what matters. What matters with mistakes is what you do afterwards. How you choose to fix it."

Thông said, slowly, "You can't understand—" and then stopped, aghast at their own daring. It'd have been funny in other circumstances. A Vanisher, looking very much like her old masters, afraid they'd disrespect her. But no, they weren't a Vanisher. Or, more accurately: they were, but they would always be, first and foremost, her own child, her and Hoang's own child, and so would Liên. "I'm sorry, Mother."

"No, you're right," Vu Côn said. "I'll never be what you are. I'll never walk in your skin. But that's the doom of all parents. And I can tell you that it goes the same way for everyone. We all stumble. We all fail. You always do the same thing: you apologize and change, again and again and again. There'll never be a place where everything is right, but we can try our best to strive towards it. It's the striving that defines us. That makes us different from them."

"Them?"

"Your genitors," Vu Côn said. She thought of Kim Ngoc, and of the villages, and of her masters' distant, fading laughter. Gone. They were gone, and couldn't touch Vu Côn or those she loved anymore. "You're not defined by your blood. It's your acts that matter, in the end."

"Mother . . ."

Vu Côn set her own tea on the table. "I'm not saying it's easy. Just that it's possible." And that, just like Thông, she would face the consequences of her own acts, of her own failure to diagnose Yên earlier.

Thông stared at her for a while, and said nothing. Which was fine. She hadn't expected an answer. Just something they could chew on.

"Can we help you?" Liên said, a little too loudly.

Vu Côn moved to the foundry bowl, and sent the command. The words shimmered silver for a fraction of a second, and then vanished as the surface of the bowl went darker. Digesting them. "This is for me to do," she said. "My own mistakes to fix."

"Mother," Thông said as the dark shapes of instruments began to appear in the bowl. Unlike the tea, it wasn't instant. The bowl was accessing the table of recommended surgeries for the diagnosis, and using that as a template to offer Vu Côn her instruments and medicine.

"Yes?"

Thông wouldn't look at her. "I don't want to be presumptuous, but—"

"Oh, do spit it out."

"I saw your diagnosis. The White Tiger, Changing." Thông's voice trailed off, and picked up again, gaining assurance as they spoke. "The symptoms don't quite match."

"I know. It's a mutation. That happens, sometimes, with viruses."

Thông took a deep breath. "It's her heartbeat. I don't like how it sounds. The White Tiger should just weaken the pulse, not make it go into syncopation like this. It doesn't even sound like a human heartbeat."

Or the heartbeat of anything that had two lungs, two sets of limbs and a set of normal organs. "I've heard it," Vu Côn said. She kept her voice even, but it cost her. "If you check the database of symptoms, you'll see some presentations of the White Tiger include arrhythmia. That's similar."

"I suppose it could be." Thông didn't look fully convinced.

"Oh, come on, big sib," Liên said. "It's not like we can claim our last operation went flawlessly."

"It was a disaster." Thông's voice was flat. "Someone died. Don't make light of it."

"Children." Vu Côn barely raised her voice. "I've told you already. We're not going to harp on responsibilities for past acts. I just want you to learn a lesson from this."

"Not trying new treatments on a patient without telling you," Liên said, automatically.

"Exactly."

In the bowl, needles and scalpels glinted, and a bottle of

disinfectant and hydrating fluids, with the darker shadow of the tools still being made by the palace. Vu Côn picked up the needles, and started sliding them, one by one, into Yên's body at the paralyzing points. "Just make sure I'm not disturbed, will you? For anyone or anything. I'll take care of the rest." And then bent, one last time, to kiss Yên on the lips: cold and unyielding, like kissing jade or marble. "It'll be over soon," she whispered.

Stop hiding things, Yên had asked, but she hadn't woken up, and there was no choice.

Vu Côn was going to make everything better.

9

In the Ruins of the World

Elder Tho hadn't changed at all.

She strode into the room where Yên was still struggling to pull herself up, her lean face suffused with that familiar arrogance. Her smile widened into the sharp, feral one of a tiger who'd found prey when she saw Yên. With her came Head Minh Phuoc, as well as five of the village's militia carrying their spears. As they came in, one of the militia effortlessly kicked Yên's legs from under her, sending her sprawling and coughing on the floor.

"The official's return," Elder Tho spat. "Honor and glory and magic."

Yên pulled herself up again. One of the militia moved to kick her. In her exhausted, emptied mind ran the words of a spell: the one she'd used earlier against evil spirits. *Spiral. Turtle's Claw. Crossbow. Fortress.* Again and again and again, but all she could do was bow her head, completely drained of energy.

"Enough," Elder Tho said, to the militia. "Don't get carried away." Her gaze raked the room, Mother and Oanh and Elder Giang, all clustered in the small space, and stopped at Giang. "You've been spending too much time with them, younger pibling. Looking for atonement?"

Giang's gaze was drawn and exhausted. "We've had this talk, haven't we? When I am judged, nothing I do will convince the Ruler of Hell to spare me. I made a promise to this child. I'm merely keeping it."

"And your promise includes breaking the village laws? You know the consequences of that," Elder Tho said. It was weighted and barbed: something she thought would cow Giang, but Giang merely stood their ground and smiled.

"There is nothing that prevents me from caring for my daughter," Mother said, sharply.

"For a sick patient who breaks the quarantine laws?" Elder Tho's voice was sharp. "Not to mention someone we already condemned."

Yên found her voice. "Gave away," she said. It rasped and hurt in her throat. "You gave me away." She felt distant, stabbing pains in her body. Like knives, sliding one by one into her spine and the inside of her thighs. Her hands opened, nerveless and almost without feeling. At her feet, darkness pooled, became the trail of Vu Côn's robes, the words shimmering in their folds. *Choking. Sleeping. Silence.* What was happening? The sickness, progressing again? Why so fast?

Elder Tho's gaze was pitying. "A life for a life," she said. "In any case, you cannot possibly have imagined we'd let you return."

Because of course this had never been about fairness, or justice. Because she could show all the magic in the world, but in the end, it would never earn her more than a brief reprieve until the magic left her. *Look at Mother.* Her healing skills barely keeping her alive, barely keeping her in Elder Tho's good graces. Because in the end, it wasn't even about usefulness. It was about the power of deciding who mattered. And there would always be someone, somewhere, who got drunk on it. Someone like Elder Tho.

Head Minh Phuoc was staring at her daughter. "Child," she said. "There is still time."

Oanh stood, defiantly, barely looking human in the dim light of the house. The planes of her nose shone beneath her translucent skin. "No. There isn't."

Head Phuoc turned, pleadingly, to Elder Tho. "She was just led astray by bad company."

Elder Tho's voice was soft. "I should think she knew exactly what she was doing." She shrugged. "But her, I can afford to spare."

Never about usefulness.

One of the militia picked Yên up like a rag doll. The world flipped, and she was staring at the floorboards, dangling like a puppet with cut strings, tired and bone-weary and drunk with despair. The others surrounded Elder Giang, Oanh and Mother.

Elder Tho said, to Mother, "Grandmother?" It was a question. Yên understood what was being offered. A chance to deny. A short reprieve until favors ran out once more.

Mother laughed. "Did you imagine this would go any other way, *child*?" She spat the words, drawing herself to her full height, as fierce and as indomitable as any dragon.

"I suppose not," Elder Tho said. She gestured. "To the Grove, then."

The purifying circle. Yên's old memories: the corona of light flaring up, word after word lighting up, and in the circle, layer after layer of Old Thanh Hoa's skin forming spinning lines like the lashes of a whip, skin and muscles and slivers of bones chipped away while the scream went on and on. An ending, of a sort. Except that Mother would die too.

More knives, this time along her hips and the outside of her legs. A brief jolt, and then the feeling in her legs disappeared too. Everything blurred and blacked out. She didn't remember being carried out of the house or through the village. They were now along the river, under the dull cover of the perpetually grey sky. They'd tied the hands of Mother, Elder Giang and Oanh, and run a rope from one to the next, like a chain of indentured people moved from village to village. The ground was thick with mold and dead leaves, so unlike the polished metal floors of Vu Côn's palace.

Vu Côn.

She could. She could call Vu Côn.

Ahead was the Plague Grove, and the shining circles traced under the skeletal trees. The sound of the river rushing by, a memory of wet lips against hers, of breathing in the sea as she lay on a bed in times now dead to her. Thông and Liên, shivering and shrinking from their Vanisher shape, and Vu Côn simply looking at them with anguish and love in her eyes . . .

Yên would rather die than see the dragon again.

But, if she didn't summon Vu Côn—if she didn't even try—they would all die.

Neither her hands nor her legs worked anymore. But her head did. She could tilt her lips as the militia walked, drawing the shape of the words, letter by painstaking letter.

Fish.

The word was barely visible: a faint exhalation, translucent and barely lighter than the ground. They'd entered the Grove now. Trees. Not the lifeless, perfect, skeletal trees of the Vanishers, but forked and complex ones, with broken-off branches and small brown fruit half-pecked by birds, with fungus on the trunks and dead leaves carried in the river. And the circle ahead, dark and silent.

The militia dumped Yên on the ground. She could hear Elder Tho speak, and then a sharp noise as the circle lit up, that familiar zooming noise that had haunted her as a child.

Gate.

Another word. Another shadow joining the first. The militia had unhooked Oanh from the chain and tied her to one of the trees. They were pushing Mother and Elder Giang toward the circle. Faster. She had to move faster.

River.

Storm.

At the edge of the circle, Mother had stopped, looking at Elder Tho. "You will leave me the dignity of dying free and on my feet," she said, icily.

Elder Tho shrugged. "As you wish." One of the militia moved to untie her hands. Head Minh Phuoc was trying to talk to Oanh, but Oanh had turned her head away and wouldn't look at her.

No.

Yên was running out of time. *Faster. Faster.*

Letter by letter, and all the while Mother was slowly being freed, slowly moving closer to a point of no return.

Faster.

Come.

The last word was small and pathetic, ill formed, its letters like a child's attempt at writing. It clustered with the others. *Fish. Gate. River. Storm. Come.*

Nothing happened. Yên slumped on the floor, coughing and coughing and trying to breathe through a throat that seemed to have slammed shut. All this for nothing and it was all going to go nowhere . . . .

Then the Plague Grove shook. The river rose like a living tower, sending oily, shimmering water everywhere. And through the gate came not one but two serpentine beings.

They weren't dragons. They were sleek and lethal, all teeth and legs and claws, and their presence tore the world apart. In their wake was only the silence of dead things.

No. That wasn't—that wasn't what she'd—

When they landed, the ground fractured all the way to

Yên, the earth cracking like celadon put in too much heat. One of the militia made for them, spearpoint extended toward Thông's belly. They moved, fluid and deadly, and sent them sprawling. The smaller one hesitated, but didn't continue the movement that would have speared the militia like a caught fish. The larger one's tail wrapped around Elder Tho, constricting her in coils of scales, and again and again around the militia. It looked like the chain they'd formed with Oanh, Mother and Elder Giang. It'd have been ironic, in other circumstances—poetic justice, the coils drawn tight enough to suffocate or break bones and ribcages.

Yên struggled to breathe. The knives had stopped going into her body, but the world seemed to shimmer and grow distant around her, the trees and the clouds yellowing at the edges, as if the Grove were burning. What was happening? Everything seemed to grow farther and farther away from her . . . .

"No," Mother said. She'd moved away from the circle, staring warily at the beings. At the twins, for who else could they be? The last Vanishers in the entire world.

The larger one spoke. Thông, except that their voice shook the branches of the trees and sent ripples all the way through the earth, and into the river. "They were about to kill you."

Mother didn't move.

A silence, while the world held its breath.

At length, Thông shook their head. "Fine. No matter how much you may deserve it." They spoke a word in a language that made Yên's body writhe without conscious volition. The purifying circle blinked once, twice, and then shattered. The earth moved and broke beneath it, splitting into smaller and smaller pieces until nothing of the light was left. "Go away, before I change my mind."

The coils relaxed. Neither Elder Tho nor the militia waited to be told twice. They ran away from the Grove. Head Minh Phuoc untied Oanh and stood, shaking.

The Vanishers shimmered and shrank, and the twins stood in their place. They were still half in Vanisher shape. Liên's face was framed by the thin razor blades of antlers, and Thông's robes were hiding too many limbs, too many claws.

They'd saved her life. They could have killed everyone there, but they hadn't. It didn't make sense. None of it made sense.

Yên tried to pull herself up, but her limbs kept flopping out of control. That odd yellowish tinge again. A wave of nausea, of rising vertigo, even as the cough started up again in her lungs, and she was turning her head left and right, frantically fighting to breathe.

Mother was still speaking. "I'm not the one who summoned you."

"I know you're not," Thông said. "And you didn't summon us, but Mother was really busy with something else. . . ." They stopped then, stared at Yên, horror stealing across their face. "Teacher. You can't be here. That's not possible."

Yên waited for the wave of coughing to pass. When

she opened her eyes again, Thông was kneeling in the mud, looking at her. "Teacher," they said, and their worried voice was that of the student she'd taught, back in the palace, before everything had changed.

"You—" Words didn't seem to be swimming through the morass of her mind. "You saved them."

Thông shrugged, an expansive movement that made the embroidery on their robes move like living things. "You saved Liên." They looked embarrassed, and in that moment Yên saw not a scaled monstrosity but merely a student praised for something that came naturally to them. She saw Thông's worry and fear, and Liên hovering behind them, one hand gripping her sibling's shoulder hard enough to bruise, and understood just what Vu Côn had seen in them. Not Vanishers, not her former masters, but simply *children*. Children, bewildered and lost and trying so very hard to make sense of the world that their parents had abandoned them in. "I'm sorry," she started to say, but Thông airily waved a hand.

"There's something more urgent, Teacher. How can you be here?"

"I don't understand."

"I've seen you. In the palace. You look the same, except a great deal paler and more silent." It made no sense.

"May I?" Thông moved when Yên nodded, gently lifting her from the mud of the grove, cradling her in splendored, warm brocade. "I— Mother said you needed to be healed."

The palace. Yên felt tired, so tired. Leeched of warmth,

of desire to move. "I've seen it in dreams. Your mother was carrying me into a room. . . ." She stopped. "It's not dreams, is it?"

"No." On Mother's face, on everyone's face, that same slow dawning of horror. "Two heartbeats. The echo. I've seen this before. Old Thuan, when his husband died. Part of him remained at the gravestone in the tomb, and part of him just went on like before. Two shadows, âm and duong."

"I've not heard of it," Thông said, slowly.

"We have." Liên's voice was flat. "The fisherman and the scholar."

"It's a *story*. A tale for children."

Mother snorted. "It's true. I was a young, inexperienced healer, and no one suspected anything until Thuan collapsed in the fields. Being split in two is exhausting, but it's not fatal. Unless it goes on for too long."

"That's not all she has," Giang said.

Mother's face was hard. "No. She also has Oanh's sickness, or something similar to it. *That's* what's weakening and killing her, not the split soul."

Yên struggled to speak. It took all she had. "Knives . . ." she whispered. "I could feel them, going in."

Thông's face was hard. "Not knives, teacher. Acupuncture needles."

"In the palace," Yên said, slowly. It made sense, didn't it? She could see what was happening there, and she could feel its effects, too.

Liên said, "She can feel what's happening in the palace?"

181

Aliette de Bodard

"Distantly." Mother shook her head. "It's âm duong. Each of them always carries the seed of the other within themselves."

"Healing," Yên whispered. Vu Côn, never stopping to ask her, to tell her what was going on. Or perhaps she'd told her other-self in the palace, but in all her dreams she'd been mute and unresponsive.

Healing. She didn't want to be healed. She didn't want to go on. There was no point. The village wouldn't take her, and any other village would just be the same: more fear and more worries of what would happen to her, the day they found her unworthy.

"The healing will kill you," Mother said. She'd never believed in dancing around the point with patients. "You need to heal both halves. Not doing that is just . . . like trying to put together a broken cup with only half the pieces. What Vu Côn will get will be so much less than what you started out with." Her voice didn't shake, but it took a visible effort.

Yên lay back, and stared at the clouds: swollen and grey, and branches of trees shaken like wet rags by the wind, and the sky turning darker and darker, with lighter shapes, like birds, weaving in and out of focus. More and more of them, filling up her entire field of vision. No, not birds, words. Dying. Would it be so bad?

"Can you fix it?"

"There's a procedure." Mother's voice was hard. "What we need to do first is stop your mother before it's too late."

Thông rose, carrying Yên. They held her to Elder Giang. "Here. Hold her."

They leapt and stretched and shifted, and stood upon the earth in their Vanisher shape, in the middle of a thousand dark rivulets of water as dark as blood. Elder Giang placed her in a hollow of the serpentine body, tearing out cloth from their robes to tie Yên to the spines on Thông's back. Then they stepped away, watching Thông. "Don't worry about me or Oanh," they said, and it wasn't clear if they were speaking to Yên or Mother or both. "Elder Sister Thọ's power is broken, for now. We'll find our place in the new order of the village." Their face was hard, as cutting as the edge of a sword.

Mother nodded, though she didn't look happy. Yên's vision fuzzed, and the next thing she knew, they were flying.

Nothing seemed to remain steady or oriented the same way. The air rushed around them, whistling and keening like lost souls; and then the river, murky and oily, came up to meet them. A flash of darkness, and they were flying in an unfamiliar sky, the stars scattered like wounds across the raw, angry surface, every one of them a hole in the fabric of the universe, bleeding the color of rust and rot onto the black canvas of heaven . . . .

"Stay with me, child," Mother said. Her face was hard.

Yên's field of vision was slowly filling up with words. She blinked, dispelling them, and saw instead Vu Côn's dark eyes, drawing her into their depths.

"How far?" Mother asked. Ahead was the smaller,

sleeker shape of Liên, the droplets of water in her mane shining like molten metal.

"Not long," Thông said. "Hang on."

Mother's hands on Yên's wrists. A cool, comforting touch that reminded her of being sick as a child, of being safe, even though it had always been a lie, even though diseases took children more than they took anyone else. "I trust you," Mother said.

"You'd be the first one," Thông said, with a bitter laugh.

"Doesn't your mother?"

"That's . . ." Thông was silent, for a while. "She's our mother. You're . . ."

"Human?"

"A stranger."

Mother said, "You saved my life. What else am I supposed to think of you?"

Thông said nothing in answer. They banked over a large metal structure—a sharp, serrated assemblage of towers and crenelated walls, of gardens and courtyards and spheres, rising gracefully from the dead earth—the palace. Yên had never seen it from the air. She couldn't feel anything anymore. The knives were slipping into her cheeks just below the eyes, drawing a slow, protracted line toward her lips. A further one into her mouth, pinning the tongue in place. Numbing cold spread from there, snuffing out all the words in her throat before she could utter them.

Mother, she tried to say, but nothing would hold her anymore, as Thông dived for the palace entrance and, barely waiting for the huge filigreed doors to open, flew through the frame, arrowing through the corridors that followed with dizzying, sinuous ease.

Polished metal, impossible walls. Slowly wheeling patterns of flowers whose petals tapered to long sharp points, like fingerbones stripped of flesh. Sleek birds endlessly receding into the distance, their distorted, jagged wings becoming the bodies of gigantic fish, and the eyes of the fish becoming the bodies of the birds again. Windows opening on landscapes that kept changing weather and orientation, as if a mere step could change time and space and back again. Shapes so easily, so fluidly flowing into one another, distance altering itself until it became meaningless, dizzying heights so easily becoming close enough to touch.

And, flying through it all, watching it blur and become alien and new, Yên understood, for the first time, what it meant to be a Vanisher.

They'd had everything, and everything had come easily to them: their own shapes, the mastery of bodies and minds, the magic that enabled them to reshape rivers and seas and hills with a single word. In time, they'd become like Elder Tho: drunk on their own power and seeing everything as their due. The world as nothing more than a toy to be broken, so that no one would ever enjoy what they'd had when they'd left. The people who lived with them as theirs, subjects to be experimented on, to be enslaved and put to work. A laughing, running child only as a life that could be molded to suit their own purposes.

She flew, paralyzed and mute, through the shell of their palace, what should have been the last remnant of their presence on earth; and she understood that they had never really left. That they all—humans, spirits, even the constructs—lived in the palaces the Vanishers had built.

It wasn't just the broken world that the Vanishers had left behind. They'd left, too, their true victory: the standards by which people treated each other. Seeing limited resources as things to fight for, people as bodies to safeguard the villages, the old and sick as needless burdens. Weighing everyone against necessity and survival. Even Elder Giang could only see Elder Tho's downfall as a change of powers.

Except Mother, who refused to play by the rules even if it killed her. And . . .

And Vu Côn.

Vu Côn was arrogant and cocksure, and she treated Yên like a child. She treated everyone, twins included, like a child, and would probably think Mother was some kind of charming primitive.

But she'd taken on two Vanisher children and had raised them, never asking them for their magic or their powers. She hadn't even wanted Thông to bespeak the palace, and it had been Liên's life at stake, back then. In the end, no matter how many constraints she'd placed on them, she'd left that decision to Thông. She'd freed Yên and expected nothing in return, only given Yên the choice of where she wanted to go next. Through it all, Vu Côn had striven, however infuriatingly, to do what was right.

It changed nothing. It meant nothing. She had to remember this. She—

Thông flew on. Gardens and courtyards, and towers that became chasms. The garden where she'd taught the twins, with its solitary tower. Ahead, Liên dived into an open space filled with fluted pillars, and Thông followed. As they dived, the pillars twisted, but the garden remained. Yên realized, with a peculiar lurch, that the door ahead of them was also a window in the stretched tower that stood in the center of the garden. It shouldn't have been possible, but she was dying, and what did it matter what the palace was throwing at her?

Yên found only growing nausea within her—part of her flying, banking wildly and dangerously with Thông's reckless trajectory, the other part still and silent on the operating table—and neither could move or talk or say anything. Ahead, Liên spoke, and her words made the palace shake. The impossible door trembled, and split open like a ripe fruit, bleeding golden dust upon the floor. And then they were through, into what lay behind.

Inside was only shadow. A dark silhouette standing by a table, holding something that gleamed. Thông slid to a stop, coils coming up to cushion Yên's fall as she rolled off their body. And Mother pulled herself up from the landing as if nothing was amiss, and stood upright, saying, quietly and forcefully, "Elder Aunt. Stop. Now."

10

The Next Breath

Vu Côn had been so focused on the operation, delaying that inevitable moment when she'd have to sink knives into Yên's flesh, opening her belly up like a bloodied flower, that anything else had barely registered. When the summoning spell rang through the palace, she dimly noted that the twins had left, and turned back to cooling the coins she'd need to apply to Yên's sides.

Then someone spoke outside the room, and the floor under Vu Côn split itself apart as if in the middle of an earthquake. She danced over the cracks with a coin in her hand, muffling a swear as the coldness of the coin sank into her skin. This one was wasted and she'd have to do it again. She—

The twins. That voice didn't belong to Thông, so it had to be Liên. What—

The door had slammed open. Two Vanishers flew through. A smaller, unfamiliar shape, followed by the larger one of Thông, who slid to a halt—and, clambering from their back like a woman decades younger, Kim

Ngoc, walking toward Vu Côn with absolutely no fear on her face. "Elder Aunt. Stop. Now."

"You don't understand," Vu Côn started. And then stopped. Behind Kim Ngoc, Thông was shifting shapes, back to their genderless human body in scholar's robes. And, as they rose from the floor, they held Yên in their arms.

Vu Côn turned to look at the operating table. The still, pale shape of Yên, lying unconscious with the needles at the various paralysis points. She turned again. In Thông's arms, a second Yên dangled, arms and legs completely limp.

No.

"Yên was the one who summoned us," Thông said. "She said she could feel the needles you were sliding into her." Their face was expressionless, but talking cost them an effort. They were reproaching their own mother.

"There's a story," Kim Ngoc said. She faced Vu Côn, much as her daughter had once faced a dragon. "About a person who left his shadow-self with the Vanishers, and his lover's quest to rescue him."

"It's . . ." Vu Côn forced herself to speak. "It's a story."

"So are dragons." Kim Ngoc's face didn't move.

Vu Côn's fingers trailed on the operating table, took Yên's pulse. She heard that odd, arrhythmic beat; and with absolute certainty she knew it to be not one, but two heartbeats mingled together. She looked from Thông to her operating table, from Yên to the other, ghostly Yên. Am duong, the two selves entwined in a human body. One half of each. "I can heal her," she said.

"Not like this," Kim Ngoc said. "You can't heal half a person."

A flash of anger, as cold as the depths of the sea. "You don't know anything. You're—" She was just a small healer in a small village, struggling to survive, and what would she know of the human body?

But Thông was holding Yên's other-self, her shadow-self, her broken soul. And Vu Côn's fingers, still on Yên's pulse, could hear that echoing heartbeat.

She'd been wrong. Her diagnosis had been wrong. Her planned cure had been wrong, and the wrong cures were death.

She'd ignored the warning signs. She'd been so confident she could fix things, she'd browbeaten Thông into silence, and she'd ignored the call the twins had answered, the one that had brought half of Yên back into the palace. She'd thought it was a choice between doing nothing and letting Yên die, but it wasn't that, not at all.

Because she hadn't stopped. Because she'd been so convinced she was right, she'd almost killed or maimed Yên.

Stop hiding things. Stop making the decisions for me.
Stop.
I want to know.

She'd stumbled and failed, and she could go on and on and pretend everything was fine. Or she could follow her own advice, and strive to make things right.

Thông had said Yên had summoned the twins. Which meant that some part of her had been awake, at some point. Before the operation had started. Who knew if she would wake up. But that wasn't the point. The point was that Vu Côn would stop making excuses for herself.

"Will you—" She took a deep, shaking breath, and said to Kim Ngoc, "Will you help me heal her? Please?"

Kim Ngoc's smile was tight. "I can try, if she's not too far gone. I can put both halves back together. But you need to wake her up now."

Vu Côn slid the acupuncture needles from Yên's body, one by one. And then stood back, and waited.

In Thông's arms, Yên stirred. Her body arched once, twice, flopping back weakly. Vu Côn forced herself not to run to her. Thông knelt, putting her on the floor, gently propping her up. Her eyes opened. Her gaze slowly focused, and she looked straight at Vu Côn. "Elder sister," she whispered. "You—" She closed her eyes again, leaning on Thông. "Hiding things," she whispered. "I told you—"

On the operating table lay Yên's duong-self, silent and unconscious, paler than she was. Duong, the dormant fires, the scorched earth that only needed shade and water to come alive again. "You were right," Vu Côn said. "It should be your choice, not mine." She walked slowly, unsteadily, toward Yên, knelt by Thông's side so that she would no longer tower over her. She was half in dragon shape again—antlers and scales, and her tail lengthening beneath her robes—as she always was when under stress. The floor was cool and cold to her touch, steadying her. "Just tell me what you want."

* * *

Yên hadn't expected the question, and she hadn't expected it coming from Vu Côn. No one had asked. Not even the twins or Mother. Everyone had been so caught up in the heat of the moment, of trying to get her to the palace before it was too late. But even before that, there had been no time.

Or had that just been excuses she was making for herself?

Her vision was still swimming. Now that she was in the same room as her other-self, she could feel a dull tug in her legs, a sense something else was there that she ought to take a look at. But nothing that would banish the all-encompassing weariness in her legs.

Tell me what you want.

"I don't know," she whispered. "I don't know."

Vu Côn's hands held her, cold and steadying. "It's all right. You don't have to."

"You don't understand. I don't— I can't—" She thought of flying through the Vanishers' Palace, of that moment of understanding like an awakening, that they all lived in the ruin of a world the Vanishers had made. All of them, except the people who now surrounded her. Vu Côn. The twins. "I can't go back."

Vu Côn was silent, for a while. "I made you an offer, once. You can still stay in the palace. You too," she said, to Mother. A slow, amused laugh. "I guess we could use other healers here."

"Child. You're running out of time." Mother's voice

was matter-of-fact. "It's not really a choice, Yên. You saw Oanh. She would have died."

"It *is* a choice," Vu Côn's voice was almost gentle. "Everything is. Yên?"

She wanted to live, because who would choose to die? And yet . . . Mother had Oanh and Elder Giang, so it wasn't even as if she was indispensable anymore. The same chasm she'd seen once yawned under her feet. A world where she didn't have the safety of returning to the village, to any village, anymore, where her life wasn't the slow wait for the elders to cast her out, where there seemed to be no roads to the future.

Vu Côn bent, and slowly, carefully kissed her. A surge of cold on Yên's lips, the river that took her, that saw every measure of her body and still rose to drown her, that same slow rise of desire, hardening her spine and breasts. For a moment—a brief, exhilarating moment, she was on her back in the bed in her room, watching the dragon towering over her—feeling coils wrap around her legs, and the wave of desire that had crested in her then, that simple moment of slaking her thirst, of *breathing* after so long spent choking.

"That's—" Yên fought to speak. "That's not an answer." It couldn't possibly be one.

Vu Côn simply kissed her again. Yên's lips felt twice too large for her face: that same pleasant numbness, stealing over her and making her whole.

Vu Côn said, "Of course not. No. It never is. But you take the future as you take everything else: one step at a time. What do you want, Yên?"

The palace. The hospital. The twins and Mother, helping. And Vu Côn and everything they hadn't said to each other, all the pathways into the future. She thought of the river and the dragon rising from the heart of it, sleek and shining and so *beautiful*. Of what it had felt like, to run away from the palace in the wake of the one night they had spent together. Of reading the book and learning how magic worked. That heady feeling of understanding how things worked, of words coming alive and singing for her in the dark of the night, much as the scholars of old had once pored over books to write their own life-shattering poems.

You need to care a little more about yourself and your own happiness.

She wanted to say that too many things separated her and the dragon, that it wouldn't last, but then she understood that Vu Côn was right. It didn't matter. She didn't need a pathway into the future, or a road that took her years ahead, all the way to old age.

She just needed a reason to take the next breath.

She reached out, arms trembling with the effort, pulled Vu Côn to her: no kiss this time, but merely holding the dragon against her, feeling Vu Côn's rapid heartbeat, the panic and fear she wasn't showing. Feeling the coldness of her, the dampness of the river and the storms, washing over her, taking her whole.

"Please," she said, to Vu Côn. "Help me."

* * *

She'd not been sure, before Mother and Vu Côn put her to sleep, that she would ever wake up.

But she did, and found herself in her old room. The infinitely receding walls felt almost familiar, almost comforting. The bed was warm and soft, and there were two Vanishers perched on the end of it, with no regard whatsoever for privacy.

"She's awake!"

"She can hear you, you know." Thông's voice was darkly amused. "Hello, Teacher."

"How—"

"It went well," Vu Côn said, from the door. The dragon stood leaning against the doorframe, sleek and elegant and perfect, her face once more a mask.

"Mother?"

"She's resting. She's not a young woman anymore, and putting you back together exhausted her." A pause, then: "How are you feeling?"

Drained, and feeling as if she'd gone through her own version of the purifying circle, as if it had sliced her into ten thousand pieces and put her back together. She took a deep breath. It didn't hurt. That was almost surprisingly wrong. She moved, and saw a faint, black shadow move on the floor, almost disconnected from her.

"The virus that was killing you is gone, but your soul is still split," Vu Côn said. "You can be in several places at once if you want, though it'll be difficult to control, and it'll exhaust you. I can stitch it back together for you, but it's a long and complex operation. I didn't want to take the responsibility of changing you." She raised a hand. "You don't have to tell me now."

"It's rather cool, actually," Liên said.

"Lil' sis." Thông snorted. And, to Yên: "It's perfectly fine either way. And you'll get better if you don't overdo it. Mother?"

"Yes?"

"Which patient were we supposed to look at? In the sleeping berths?"

Vu Côn shrugged. "You're old enough to make your own decisions, aren't you?"

A silence. Then Thông said, "If that's acceptable."

Vu Côn shook her head, forcefully. "You're adults now. Go take your own responsibilities."

Thông rose, dragging their sister with them. The shadow of sharp, skeletal antlers hung in the air as they did so. "Come on. We're just preventing Yên from resting."

"I'm not—" Yên said, and then her gaze met Vu Côn's, and she stopped protesting.

The doors slid shut behind the twins, and then it was just her and Vu Côn. Words rose, unbidden, into her mind. Her hands traced them before she knew what she was doing. *Fish. Gate. River. Storm. Come.* Something twisted in her chest: a thick, red thread pulsing like a blood vessel, pulling her up from the bed, toward the dragon.

Vu Côn's hands pushed her down, slowly and gently. She hadn't even seen the dragon move. The serpentine shape was on her bed now, coils wrapped over the sheet,

IN THE VANISHERS' PALACE

antlers against the headrest. "I can tell you're going to be a troublesome patient."

Yên smiled. That felt wrong too, like stretching muscles too long unused. And then the feeling passed. "The twins."

"They'll get into trouble," Vu Côn said. "But it's my fault. I can't keep them cooped up forever. It's time for them to make their own mistakes, and to fix them, too."

Yên thought of Gia Canh and the gardens, and Liên's pale face. "They could die."

Vu Côn was silent, for a while. "Yes. And they could do that even if I were watching them all the time. You're not the only one I was making too many decisions for."

"I see." Yên said.

Vu Côn laughed. "Enough about the twins. There will be time for them later, believe me. Thông has so many ideas about how the hospital should be run. How many healers we should bring from the outside world, how many patients we would triage in a given day . . . . And Liên is already busy tinkering with sleeping berths. Without patients, this time, thank Heaven. It's only a matter of time until something breaks spectacularly and we have to help them sort out the mess again." She sounded resigned rather than fearful. She leaned back against the headrest. It creaked, the wood lengthening. Words glowed, in the folds of her robe. *Duty. Family. Care.* Her eyes, searching Yên's own, were dark, and in their depths was a trembling light, like a distant lamp seen through layers of rain. Her hands, holding Yên's own, shook: that same fear Yên had felt, in the laboratory, the one Vu Côn hadn't shown to anyone else.

"It'll be all right," Yên said.

"No more hiding," Vu Côn said. "Remember? It won't be all right. It won't be normal, or easy. But that's fine."

"What happens now?"

Cold seized Yên's fingers, and descended all the way into her spine. "Everything," Vu Côn said, and her smile was dazzling.

"Everything." Yên mouthed the syllables again, felt them like saltwater on her tongue, like a spell, slowly coming together to change the ruined world they lived in. "I think I'd like that."

Acknowledgments

I would like to thank the following people:

Tade Thompson, Fran Wilde, Alis Rasmussen, Matt Wallace, Mike Headley, Rachel Monte, Liz Bourke, Likhain, Zen Cho, Vida Cruz for reading and comments, sometimes on multiple drafts!

Peter and Emma Newman for helping me have the confidence to tackle this, and Ken Liu for agreeing to be turned into a dragon.

Stephanie Burgis, Nene Ormes, Alessa Hinlo, Victor R Fernando Ocampo, Inksea, D Franklin, Zoe Johnson and Elizabeth Bear for general support.

Gareth L Powell, Jennifer Brinn, and George Cotronis for help with the blurb. To Juliet Kemp, Juliet McKenna, Michelle Sagara for general publishing advice (and Juliet Kemp for proofreading!). To Richard Shealy for very helpful and speedy copyediting.

Rhiannon Rasmussen-Silverstein, Melanie Ujimori and Kelsey Liggett for cover design and cover art.

John Berlyne, Lisa Rodgers, Patrick Disselhorst, and everyone at JABberwocky for putting together this book.

About the Author

Aliette de Bodard lives and works in Paris. She is the author of the critically acclaimed Obsidian and Blood trilogy of Aztec noir fantasies, as well as numerous short stories which have garnered her two Nebula Awards, a Locus Award and a British Science Fiction Association Award.

Her space opera books include *The Tea Master and the Detective*, a murder mystery set on a space station in a Vietnamese Galactic empire, inspired by the characters of Sherlock Holmes and Dr. Watson. Recent works include the Dominion of the Fallen series, set in a turn-of-the-century Paris devastated by a magical war, which comprises *The House of Shattered Wings* (Roc/Gollancz, 2015 British Science Fiction Association Award, Locus Award finalist), and its standalone sequel *The House of Binding Thorns* (Ace, Gollancz).

Visit her website www.aliettedebodard.com for free fiction, Vietnamese and French recipes and more.